*He moved closer, drawing her toward him.*

*As if mesmerized Serafina could not resist.*

*"Would it be too difficult for you to pretend to love me, Serafina?" he asked in a soft, persuasive voice.*

*She looked up into his face, so close to hers. "Any woman would be proud to love you," she whispered.*

*Her lips were ready when his gently met hers. He could not mistake her response, and he was smiling as he drew away from her a few moments later.*

*"There now, you underestimate your own ability, my dear. You pretend admirably well."*

Also by Rachelle Edwards
*Published by Fawcett Crest Books:*

MARYLEBONE PARK
LOVE FINDS A WAY
RAKE'S REVENGE
THE HIGHWAYMAN AND THE LADY
LUCIFER'S LADY
SWEET HOYDEN
RUNAWAY BRIDE
LADY OF QUALITY
THE RANSOME INHERITANCE
REGENCY MASQUERADE
AN UNEQUAL MATCH
DANGEROUS DANDY
THE SCOUNDREL'S DAUGHTER
THE MARRIAGE BARGAIN
FORTUNE'S CHILD

# LORD TRENTON'S PROPOSAL

Rachelle Edwards

FAWCETT CREST • NEW YORK

A Fawcett Crest Book
Published by Ballantine Books


Library of Congress Catalog Card Number: 90-93577

ISBN 0-449-21869-4

Manufactured in the United States of America

First Edition: April 1991

# ONE

"It's so exciting to know we are going to London at last, after so much planning, not to mention the false starts," Miss Imogen Geddes sighed as she sank back into the comfortable squabs of her father's traveling carriage.

The last staging post had just been left behind, and the two passengers were well on their way to London.

Imogen Geddes's blue eyes were bright with anticipation as she silently contemplated the treats to come, peering at frequent intervals out of the curtained window, squeaking excited comments to her companion. She was dressed in a fashionable gown of chartreuse satin, and a few fair curls escaped the brim of her poke bonnet, which was tied becomingly with a large satin bow. As with most young ladies of her age, she was fully aware of how fetching was her countenance, but she was not overly conceited about her fair looks, which was a fault in so many of her contemporaries.

"However," she added with a soft chuckle, "I shall be prodigiously relieved when we are past Hounslow Heath. Before we left Coverdale, Lydia

Humphreys related to me the most alarming tales of what had befallen travelers on the road."

"You need not fear highwaymen or footpads, Imogen," her companion assured her. "Horse patrols have driven them off this particular stretch of road, and if that is not sufficient to set your mind at rest, Sir Donald has provided us with enough outriders to see off the most persistent tobyman."

Imogen Geddes's companion, Miss Serafina D'Arblay, was several years her senior, a handsome woman of some five and twenty. Her hands were set neatly on her lap, cosily ensconced in a velvet muff. Her very stillness was a direct contrast to Imogen, who frequently fidgeted in her seat when she was not peering out of the window. Serafina was gowned rather less fashionably than the younger girl, even dowdily in dun-colored velvet, the style of which was several years out of date. However, she did contrive to wear her clothes with an unconcious style, which often gave strangers the impression she possessed rather more consequence than was actually so.

"Sorry as I am that Mama was not well enough to accompany me, Serafina, it will be much jollier, I feel, to have you by my side. It was quite a bright idea, you must own, to have you accompany me in her stead, even though you did, at first, resist the suggestion."

Serafina smiled in a conciliatory manner. "I did not demur to be disobliging, only I felt that I was not equipped to be a companion, and I had no desire to go to London. However, I confess to being glad I was persuaded to change my mind. I am content to be of service to you and your parents in whatever fashion they wish."

"I'm persuaded it will be a most pleasant change for you, after being so bound up in Papa's library for all this time."

"Being an archivist is most interesting, I assure you."

"I cannot possibly conceive of that. However, as you have chosen to work in that manner, I dare-say you must truly think so."

"Oh, do look, Imogen, this must be the toll at Knight's Bridge. It cannot be long before we arrive at Lady Wolcot's house. I declare *I* am beginning to be excited now!"

"It was fortunate for me that she offered to bring me out after Mama became ill. I should have hated to have been obliged to wait for another year, when I would, no doubt, be considered a trifle too old for a come-out Season."

Serafina eyed her with amusement but said entirely seriously, "I'm persuaded Lady Wolcot had that in mind when she invited you."

"Mama's indisposition might even prove to be a blessing in disguise, not that I would wish any harm to her, naturally," she added with a laugh. "But my godmother is quite a *grande dame* of the *ton* and rather influential in elevated circles. I am most fortunate to have Lady Wolcot as my god-mother."

"Have you seen her in recent years?" Serafina asked, displaying true interest.

"Not since I was a very small child in leading strings. Lady Wolcot dislikes country living, and

Mama and Papa have rarely gone up to London in recent years. Mama's health has been so indifferent, and you know full well how tedious Papa finds London, although I cannot for anything conceive why. All the diversions Mama has described to me seem sublime, and you are bound to enjoy them, too."

"I daresay I shall only be called upon to accompany you when her ladyship is unable," Serafina pointed out.

"I shall insist that you join all our expeditions. You are, after all, not a servant, and I will not for anything have you treated as one."

"It is kind of you to say so, but I do not in the least mind remaining at Wolcot House while you and her ladyship enjoy all the diversions available to a debutante. No doubt she possesses a fine library, which will keep me happy in your absence."

"Tush! You will not, on this occasion, lose yourself in anyone's library. Since you have been at Coverdale cataloging all Papa's papers, I have come to look upon you as a friend."

Serafina turned to her, smiling, taking one hand from her muff and placing it over the girl's. "How it warms my heart to hear you say so, my dear, and I confess I feel similarly attached to you. However, I'm persuaded Lady Wolcot will look upon me as the paid employee that I am, and quite rightly so. When I lived at Coverdale, I found myself in a most congenial situation, and I have no doubt whatsoever the same will be said of Wolcot House while I am there with you. Your Mama and Papa have charged me with the task of accompanying you whenever necessary during your first Season in London, and that I shall do with the greatest of pleasure, but I also have no doubt at all that your godmother will wish to accompany you as much as is possible so she is able to renew her acquaintance with you."

Imogen's eyes sparkled at the mention of her coming debut. "I have heard a great deal of what I may expect during the coming Season, and Lady Wolcot wrote to me with the information that she has been compiling a list of possible suitors. The thought of it is so exciting. Imagine! All those exceedingly eligible young men paying court to *me*, Imogen Geddes."

Gazing out of the window, Serafina's eyes clouded suddenly. "You did once, not long ago, declare everlasting devotion to Jolyon. Do you recall?"

The girl's cheeks took on a pinkish hue. "Naturally I do. I shall always remain fond of your brother, you may be sure, Serafina, but you must appreciate it was nothing more than calf love. Papa would never countenance such a match. Jolyon has always known that as well as I. He is all but penniless with no prospects for the future."

"He remains devoted to you," Serafina pointed out, her heart aching for her brother, whose anguish of late, knowing that Imogen was to go to London to find a suitable husband, had been dreadful to see.

"A gentleman as fine as Jolyon D'Arblay is certain to win the heart of some suitable female before long. What I would like to do during our stay in London is find a suitable match for *you*."

Serafina's head jerked around, her eyes wide, a smile of astonishment on her lips. "For me?"

"Yes, why not? No one denies you are handsome, my dear."

"There are others who are more handsome with the added advantages of fortune and youth."

"You are only five and twenty. No one can deny your connections are impeccable. All you lack is a portion, and there must be many gentlemen, widowers, and the like who would be glad with you as a wife. At Coverdale there was Squire Thornbury. All you needed to do was encourage him a little, but you did not."

The recollection of being pursued by the widower, who was seeking a mother for his six children, depressed Serafina, and she answered truthfully, "I'd as lief remain a spinster."

"Oh, surely not! How could you? There are such ugly names for spinsters to be whispered behind one's back. Ape-leader. Thornback. Tabby. I could not bear it said of me." Imogen shuddered as she spoke.

Serafina said, glancing at her wryly, "It's not likely that you will be called upon to suffer such an odious fate, dearest. Your future marriage is what we are here to concentrate upon; that is why we have come to London."

The girl's eyes brightened again. "Oh yes, I shall not forget that for a moment. Indeed, when the Season begins, there will be so much to do, I am certain my head will be in a constant whirl! Lady Wolcot will ensure I am invited to all the most elevated diversions, and I am persuaded she will have made certain we obtain vouchers to Almack's. Now, that is the one place you cannot expect to be admitted, Serafina. Vouchers are so difficult to obtain, it is such an honor to be allowed to attend. If I don't contrive to procure vouchers for Almack's next Season, I may as well be *dead*!"

"You may be sure that Lady Wolcot will make the greatest efforts to obtain them on your behalf."

"No doubt her ladyship numbers some of the patronesses among her closest acquaintances. Do you think we shall meet Lord Byron? It is said he goes out into society often. Ever since I read *Childe Harold's Pilgrimage* this spring—which Lady Wolcot was obliging enough to send to me—I have been in a fidge to meet him."

"I daresay it is entirely possible if, as you believe, he goes out into society, for Lady Wolcot will ensure you go only to the most fashionable assemblies."

"I have heard say that ladies often swoon in his presence, but I am determined I shall not be such a goosecap."

Both young ladies laughed, and, glancing out of the window yet again, Imogen said, "Look at those villas, Serafina. Aren't they handsome? Everyone lives very handsomely in London, I fancy."

"We must be very close to Manchester Square now. The traffic is quite heavy. I have never seen so many carriages on the road at one and the same time."

Imogen shivered with delight. "Some of them are very fine indeed. Just look at the phaeton that has passed us! I should love to ride in *that*!"

When Serafina put her head out of the window, it was to see a bright yellow carriage with wheels so high they elevated the driver's box to the level of a first-floor window. She gasped as it shot off ahead of them, only to be brought to a standstill a few yards farther on because of congestion.

"I have never seen anything like it," Serafina gasped as she sank back into the squabs. "Our stay is certainly not going to be devoid of amusement."

"Can you hear the drivers shouting to one another? How rude they are. I so enjoy driving the trap at Coverdale, but I don't believe I would dare tool the ribbons here in town."

"I don't suppose you will be obliged to, for Lady Wolcot is certain to have a number of carriages and coachmen available for your use, and when you come out, young men will be vying with each other to take you in their curricles and gigs, and those high-perch phaetons, too."

Once again the girl's cheeks grew pink. "Just now I am in a fidge to reacquaint myself with Lady Wolcot. We have corresponded over the years, but I own I have missed a closer relationship with her."

"I'm persuaded she will be more than gracious."

"Mama speaks of her constantly and tells me she was a great beauty in her youth. When they came out in the same Season, Lady Wolcot received twenty offers of marriage before she accepted Lord Wolcot's. Unfortunately, he left her a widow very soon after the wedding. She hasn't remarried, so it seems she has remained true to his memory."

Imogen drew a deep sigh at so romantic a notion and then turned to her companion once again. "I am concerned about what you will do after my Season is over. Your work at Coverdale is done, otherwise Papa would not have so readily allowed you to go. There is nothing more for you to do there, I fear."

Serafina smiled faintly. "You must not concern yourself on my behalf. I hope Sir Donald will be obliging enough to furnish me with a recommendation so that I may find another congenial post as an archivist as soon as you are settled. My one concern now is to earn sufficient to purchase Jolyon a commission in a good regiment."

Again the girl's cheeks grew pink. "He will look so handsome in the uniform of a hussar, but it will take you an unconscionable time to raise such a sum."

"Nevertheless, I will not be deflected from that course," Serafina declared, and the girl could see from the set of her chin, her friend was utterly determined.

"If you do not hurry, the war will be over. I heard Papa say only the other day Boney has made a great mistake in marching on Russia."

"Even if the war should end tomorrow, Imogen, there will always be a need for officers in the army."

At that moment, the carriage came to a halt so suddenly both young ladies were almost catapulted across to the other side of the compartment. The conveyance continued to jerk as the horses reared up in alarm. Imogen squealed in terror, and when the horses were at last calmed and the carriage no longer in any danger of overturning, she steadied herself, automatically straightening her bonnet.

While she was being thrown around the compartment, Serafina's bonnet slid back on her head, loosening her neatly arranged hair, which was usually kept back from her face and away from her neck in a severe style.

Gasping, she asked, "Imogen dearest, are you hurt?"

The girl had grown somewhat pale but managed to shake her head. "Are you?"

As Serafina put one hand to her head, another pin came loose and her hair cascaded to her shoulders. She laughed unsteadily and said, "I don't believe so."

Because the shock of what had occurred made her oblivious to her disarray, she immediately put her head out of the window to find out what had caused the problem. They had passed one overturned carriage on a rutted road during their journey, but having reached London safely, neither passenger expected to find themselves at peril now.

When she discovered herself to be trembling, Serafina took a deep breath as she peered out of the window. The road was unbelievably congested, with carriages of all sizes and types. Several drivers were tossing insults to and fro, but what had caused their near accident was immediately evident to her.

A curricle had come out of a side road, causing their own coachman to pull up sharply. At the realization of such foolhardy behavior, Serafina felt her face tighten with annoyance.

"What is happening out there?" Imogen asked. "I can see nothing from this side."

"Some idiotic driver has pulled out in front of us."

"He might have done it for a wager. Bucks often do wager on dangerous behavior."

"I cannot conceive of anyone being so crack-brained. It is becoming increasingly evident to me that driving in town is far more dangerous than braving tobymen on country roads."

Once again Serafina put her head out of the window. The offending curricle was now being very skillfully maneuvered past the carriage by its driver, whom Serafina immediately recognized to be a Corinthian. From the top of his high-crowned beaver hat to the toes of his polished Hessians, it was evident she was staring furiously at a tulip of fashion, but that did not impress her one jot.

Nor was she impressed by this late display of good driving, which it undoubtedly was, for passing between two coaches as he was attempting to do was a near-impossible task. As the curricle drew abreast of her own conveyance, the nonesuch became aware of her disdainful look, and he slowed the curricle, which she now noted was being drawn by a pair of superb, glossy-coated matched bays.

Belatedly, she noted the aristocratic escutcheon on the side of the curricle, but that did not daunt her from saying in the severest tone, "Sir, I feel bound to inform you your recklessness has caused us some considerable distress."

His eyes, which she now noted were of the deepest gray, opened wide in some surprise. Some of that surprise might well be due to her appearance. Curls trembled around her cheeks and at her shoulders, and beneath his cool, almost insolent scrutiny she became aware of it at last.

Suddenly his eyes filled with amusement, which caused her cheeks to grow hot. Then he swept off the high-crowned beaver and bowed slightly.

"I beg your pardon most heartily, ma'am. As I explained to your driver, some Jack Dandy dashed in front of me, startling my team and causing them to start forward. It is most regrettable. I trust you will suffer no lasting . . ." She thought she detected a slight twitching of his lips despite the apparent sincerity of his words. ". . . damage to your nerves. I can assure you, my driving skills rarely let me down."

"You are exceedingly boastful with little cause, sir," she retorted, stung by his manner.

"And you are delightful in dishabille, ma'am," he responded, which caused Serafina to sink back into the squabs, her cheeks turning brick red.

She snapped shut the window curtains and immediately began to tidy her hair, imprisoning it in her bonnet as the carriage set off again.

"What was all that about?" Imogen asked, looking at her curiously.

"It is all a nothing," she replied, closing her eyes and resting her head against the squabs.

How she wished she had left the matter to the

coachman. Even with her eyes tightly closed, she could not dismiss from her mind the memory of that elegant gentleman surveying her with such insolence.

# TWO

When they arrived at Wolcot House in Manchester Square a short time later, Serafina still felt rather unnerved, although she was puzzled as to the reason. They were entirely unhurt, and the man's rudeness was of no account. No doubt he considered he was being gallant to speak to her in so bold a manner. Imogen, in direct comparison, and uncharacteristically, had quickly recovered her spirits and peered out at the splendid frontage of Lady Wolcot's house in awe.

"Did you ever see such a fine establishment?"

There were shiny brass lamps at either side of the front door, which sported a lion's-head door knocker. The coachman rapped it, and moments later, two liveried footmen let down the carriage steps and escorted them into the circular hall. Soaring marble pillars led the eye to a fine atrium, and between the pillars nestled marble statuary and paintings of Wolcot ancestors in various shades of fashion. A twin stairway curved up to the first floor, and a wrought-iron balcony encircled two more. Hanging from the ceiling far above was a Venetian glass chandelier sporting countless candles, all ready to be lit.

"Allow me to introduce myself, madam," one of the lackeys said to Serafina, as a number of others began to carry their boxes up the stairs. "I am Popplewell, her ladyship's house steward. Her ladyship charges me to welcome you to her house and will receive you in the red drawing room, prior to dinner, in an hour's time."

After all this had been addressed to her, Serafina replied, "I am Serafina D'Arblay, Miss Geddes's companion."

The house steward acknowledged her words with a slight inclination of his head and then began to lead the way up the stairs.

Imogen could scarcely suppress her excitement. "I am most impressed," she whispered to Serafina as they followed the lackey up the stairs. "I wonder if all the *ton* houses are as fine as this one. As I recall a little of what Mama has told me, I fancy some might even be finer."

The bedchamber they were ushered into was a spacious one, sumptuously furnished with a large half-tester bed draped in gold brocade and thick Turkey carpets on the floor. Two windows overlooked the garden at the back of the house, and when Serafina considered that the house was situated in the heart of London, she was amazed at how peaceful was its setting.

One of the housemaids was already hard at work unpacking all Imogen's belongings from several boxes and trunks. "I daresay Lady Wolcot plans to have an entirely new modish wardrobe made for me," the girl confided. "At least, that is what she intimated in her last communication."

"It will certainly be necessary for you to have many more clothes than you possess at present," Serafina replied. "You will undertake many more engagements than you ever did at Coverdale."

Imogen chuckled at the thought just as Popplewell said, "If you will follow me, Miss D'Arblay, I will show you to your room, which is on the next floor."

Immediately Imogen looked dismayed. "The next floor? Oh, dear. I did so hope you would be given a room next to mine, with a communicating door, so we can enjoy a coze."

"We must not question Lady Wolcot's domestic arrangements, dearest. No doubt if there was a room available near to yours, it would have been allocated to me. As it is, I cannot be situated too far away from you." Imogen remained none too happy, and Serafina added cheerfully, "I shall come back for you in an hour's time, and we can go down to dinner together."

The house steward led Serafina along the balcony and up the second, narrower flight of stairs, which she suspected led to the servants' quarters. Understandably the room allocated to her was rather smaller than Imogen's, and more sparsely furnished, but adequate for her modest needs. It was, however, a far cry from her comfortable bedchamber in the Geddes's household, although in mitigation she acknowledged at Coverdale there must have been far more rooms available than here in Manchester Square, however handsome the house.

Serafina threw her reticule on the bed and walked across to the window, which was set high in the wall. The only way she was able to look out of it was by standing on the tips of her toes.

The house steward cleared his throat. "Shall I send a housemaid to help you with your unpacking, madam?"

At this moment Serafina belatedly recalled his presence and turned on her heel to bestow upon him a smile. "Oh no, that won't be necessary. I thank you, Popplewell. I can contrive well enough on my own."

"Hot water is on its way, so if there is nothing else . . ."

"Nothing," she answered cheerfully. "You've been exceedingly helpful, and I'm certain you have countless duties to attend to without wasting any more of your precious time upon me."

She took a sixpence out of her reticule and pressed it into his hand. A few minutes later Popplewell was telling Jayestone, the under footman, that it had been a long time since a lady of Miss D'Arblay's quality had visited Wolcot House, and it was a crying shame she was so reduced in circumstances to be obliged to act as companion to a slip of a girl. He expressed a hope that once Lady Wolcot made her acquaintance, she would find Serafina more fitting quarters, seeing there were several empty bedchambers on the main floor.

Meanwhile Serafina was removing her bonnet and pelisse, which she carefully placed in the press. Her clothes, of necessity, had to last as long as was possible, and she always took the greatest care of them, darning stockings and mending gloves as much as was practical without making her appear too shabby. It would have been a wicked waste to spend money on fripperies, in her opinion, when every spare shilling could be saved for Jolyon's future.

Whenever she thought about her brother and his love for Imogen, her heart ached, although she acknowledged, as he was bound to do, that a girl of Imogen's breeding and considerable fortune was meant for a man of a higher standing in society than Jolyon D'Arblay.

Unconsciously, her thoughts conjured up the memory of the gentleman in the curricle with his aristocratic escutcheon and air of authority. A gentleman Jolyon would admire and no doubt call a great gun. She drew a sigh as she glanced about her Spartan surroundings once again. Life in London was definitely going to be quite different than what had gone before, for Imogen as well as herself.

After carefully putting away her belongings, including a number of her favorite books, Serafina pulled a stool up to the window so she could more easily peer out. Her view was not of the garden, but the square at the front of the house. By now she was not at all surprised to discover carriages rattling along constantly. The noise was something she could not have imagined while she lived at Coverdale. Rising above the constant clatter of carriage wheels was the frequent cry of various peddlers who plied their wares from house to house. This noise was something else to which she would be obliged to grow accustomed. The evening hush at Coverdale or at her aunt's house nearby, was broken only by the occasional hoot of an owl or cry of a creature in the nearby wood. This would soon only be a memory.

For the first time in an age she thought about her parents and how different life might have been if they had lived. Serafina did not suppose they would have been in any way affluent, but life would have been happier. She recalled quite clearly that their family had been a happy one all those years ago, far more than some of the wealthy families she had observed.

Serafina had always held up her parents as a prime example of true love and long ago determined she would not settle for less, for her parents' romance was truly heroic in her mind. Her pretty, delicate mama, who was the daughter of a wealthy landowning family, went against parental wishes and married the young, penniless archivist who had come to catalog her father's documents.

The disapproving relatives remained unforgiving to this day, and Serafina knew that she and Jolyon were accepted as a part of the family only on sufferance. Only an existing family trust had ensured that the D'Arblay offspring had not suffered too great a hardship after their parents' deaths, a boon to Serafina, who wanted only to earn her own keep and support her brother until he was able to provide for himself.

A sound in the doorway made her step off the stool, and as she did so, a maid came into the room bearing a pitcher of hot water. It looked to be so heavy; Serafina hurried to help her place it on the washstand.

"This is so welcome," she confided. "Traveling is such a dusty business."

"If you want for anything else, ma'am, you've only to let me know. M'name's Maisie, and I share the room next door with one of the kitchen maids."

"You have sufficient to occupy your day without concerning yourself with me."

"Her ladyship keeps us all on our toes and no mistake, but as I said, if you want for anything, you just send for me. Mr. Popplewell says you're to be looked after." As she started to leave the room, the girl added, "I'll see that a hot brick's put in your bed tonight, ma'am."

Serafina smiled her thanks, and as soon as Maisie had left, she undressed and proceeded to wash away the grime of the journey. A small looking glass was propped up on a table in the corner of the room, and she caught sight of her pale face as she dried herself with the soft cotton towel. Despite being accommodated in the servants' quarters, she suspected she had been given a few little luxuries not available to them, such as soft towels and perfumed soap.

Her hair, hastily neatened in the carriage, had become loose again with the removal of her bonnet, and now it was unrestrained, reaching almost to her waist. The gentleman in the curricle had seen her like this with her hair in an unkempt halo about her face and shoulders, her cheeks pink and her brown eyes wide.

After a moment she looked away from the mirror

in confusion, not understanding why she had not immediately forgotten about the incident. No doubt that was because it was her first encounter in London. She supposed when other incidents occurred, and she met more and more people in the months to come, the memory of that insolent man about town would fade from her mind. She fervently hoped that would happen sooner rather than later, for she had no wish to keep the humiliating incident in the forefront of her mind.

Serafina quickly and deftly pinned up her unruly chestnut locks into the demure style she had adopted since leaving Miss Prudom's Academy for the Daughters of Quality. Fortunately her Aunt Wyndham had given her a parcel of unwanted and outdated gowns that Serafina easily adapted for her own, rather slimmer, frame, so she was able to choose a not too unbecoming gown in amber-colored satin in which to make the acquaintance of Lady Wolcot.

Lady Wolcot was a faithful widow and a leader of the *haute ton*, confidante of royalty, and an inspiration to all who were privileged to know her. Like Imogen, Serafina had heard this from the lips of Lady Geddes at frequent intervals and looked forward to hearing all the latest news and gossip from Lady Wolcot's pen whenever one of her all too rare communications arrived at Coverdale.

Satisfied at last that she looked presentable, Serafina made her way down to Imogen's room to find the girl being hooked into a white muslin gown with a pink sash that Serafina thought made her look like an ingenuous child.

"How do I look?" Imogen immediately asked.

"Quite ravishing," she answered truthfully, for with her blue eyes and fair curls, which had been recently cropped in the most fashionable style, she was quite beautiful.

Her beauty, coupled with her portion, would ensure her success in the coming Season. There would be no difficulty in her making an elevated match, the knowledge of which both pleased and saddened Serafina. When Imogen made her final choice, Jolyon would be heartbroken. Were it not for his lack of prospects, he and Imogen were so well suited. Serafina could not for anything visualize Imogen married to a sophisticated pink of the *ton*, and yet that was bound to be her fate. She would undoubtedly be looked upon to manage huge establishments both here and in the country. That would satisfy Sir Donald and Lady Geddes, but would it suit their daughter? Serafina wondered.

"I wasn't certain this particular gown would be suitable. . . ." Imogen ventured, casting her friend a beseeching look.

"It is perfect for one who is about to make her debut."

The girl relaxed somewhat then, but when the maidservant began to dress her hair, Imogen insisted, "I want Miss D'Arblay to do it, Lizzie. She knows exactly how I like it."

The maidservant withdrew, and Serafina began to brush through the fair curls.

"I am so excited and yet apprehensive at the same time about this evening," Imogen confided. "I do so hope Lady Wolcot approves of me."

"Why should she not?"

"I don't know, but she is so sophisticated she might find me a ninnyhammer—or worse, a clumperton."

Serafina laughed gently. "What humbug, Imogen. Just be your own self and all will be well, I assure you. No one could possibly take you in dislike."

As she put down the brush, Imogen turned to her. "I'm more than ever glad it is you who are here with me. Mama would have fussed so much, I'd have been in the hips by now. What would I do without you?"

"You would very naturally contrive" was Serafina's reply, although she was moved by the girl's declaration.

"Well, I am relieved not to have to contrive without you, dearest." As she snatched up a silk shawl threaded with silver, Imogen went on, her chatter not really hiding her nervousness. "I really am bird-witted not to ask if your room is satisfactory."

"Indeed it is. I am situated at the far side of the house, which I find most interesting, for I can watch all the comings and goings in the square from my window!"

"This room is quite lavish, don't you think?"

"Lady Wolcot has certainly done you proud," Serafina admitted, "but I confess I expected no less."

Imogen cast Serafina a sheepish glance. "I daresay we cannot delay going down any longer for fear of being late and making her ladyship angry with me on my first day in London."

"I cannot conceive why you should wish to delay

at all, dearest. Lady Wolcot is no ogre as you well know."

Once again the girl smiled faintly. "You are, as always, so full of good sense, Serafina. Once I am married, I have made up my mind to make my first priority finding you a suitable match."

"That is, if I may say so, an absurd aspiration. Once you are taken up with the social round, you will have many other, more pressing, priorities, my dear. I beg of you, do not concern yourself on my behalf as I believe I have already counseled you. If I am able to find congenial employment, I shall be satisfied well enough."

As they walked slowly down the curved staircase, Imogen looked troubled. "It is evident to me you are intent upon sacrificing any hope you have of future happiness for Jolyon's sake."

"Oh, I beg of you not to think so, Imogen. It is not only my concern for Jolyon that makes me reluctant to consider marriage. Marriage for one of my situation is not easy to achieve, and I really have no desire to enter into that state unless I happen to fall in love, and I foresee little chance of my doing so."

The girl threw back her head and laughed. When she replied, it was with a sophisticated air that dismayed Serafina and made her feel that she was the ingenue. "Oh, you must stop reading all those gothic romances of Mrs. Radcliffe's, Serafina. There are other considerations when it comes to marriage. Love is the least of it."

"Not for me," Serafina replied after hesitating a moment. "Mama never regretted choosing Papa, despite all the hardships they were obliged to endure. It is of no account in any event, for I have never met any gentleman toward whom I have harbored the slightest fondness."

Two burly footmen on duty outside the red drawing room entered by double doors set in a pillared portico. As the lackeys opened the doors, Imogen could be seen to stiffen noticeably, and she cast a beseeching look in Serafina's direction before they both went inside.

# THREE

The room had earned its name well. The walls were papered in scarlet brocade, the many pieces of Louis Quinze furniture upholstered in red silk. To add to the utter richness of the room, every piece of wood was covered in gold leaf.

Lady Wolcot was seated near the fire in a high-backed chair from which she could observe anyone who entered the drawing room. From the far side of the room, Serafina noted that she was adorned as richly as the room, in an ornate gown of cloth of gold, emphasizing her ample curves. Around her neck was a heavy collar of diamonds, matching the tiara nestling in her rather matted curls.

Once inside the room Imogen had faltered slightly, but Serafina gave her an encouraging push so that when Lady Wolcot said, "Come along in, my dear," she did hurry forward at last. "It's a long time since I last saw you, and I'm in a fidge to make your acquaintance."

Serafina remained near the door as Imogen made her curtsy to her godmother, who raised her quizzing glass to inspect her more thoroughly.

"I am so happy to be here at last, my lady," Imogen told her in a breathless voice, "and I am indebted to you for your condescension."

"How is your dear mama?" the countess inquired as she continued to inspect Imogen.

"She is considerably recovered from her indisposition, my lady, and charges me to convey her very best wishes to you."

"What a pity it is she was unable to accompany you at this particular time, but she was always delicate, I recall. However, it is unfortunate but cannot be helped. I am bound to say you have become quite lovely, my dear," she pronounced at last. "I am well pleased with you. It makes my task easier."

Serafina began to feel slightly uneasy. It was as if Imogen was being looked upon as a commodity to be sold to the highest bidder. Immediately she realized that it was foolish to find that thought in the least disturbing, for it was evident Imogen had come to London in order to make the very best marriage her fortune, position, and beauty could achieve. Otherwise she could just as well have stayed at Coverdale and married Jolyon.

"Allow me to introduce Miss Serafina D'Arblay, who has accompanied me to London, my lady," Imogen said looking a little more relaxed.

Serafina came forward at last and curtsied. When she straightened up, it was to find herself being quizzed in her turn with that same thoroughness. While being closely scrutinized, Serafina had time to likewise consider her hostess.

Lady Wolcot might well have once been a great beauty, but she was now definitely overblown, her features having coarsened with age and perhaps considerable indulgence, something that had not happened to her contemporary, Lady Geddes.

At last the countess let the quizzing glass fall again. "You, at least, are not what I expected."

One of Serafina's eyebrows rose a little. "I do beg your pardon, my lady."

The countess waved one pudgy hand in the air. "Oh, do sit down, both of you. My neck aches from looking up at you."

Obediently the two young ladies seated themselves side by side facing her on a sofa.

"A companion, in my opinion—and I have observed many—should be considerably older, and married or widowed. You are scarce older than Imogen."

"I am five and twenty, ma'am, and I regret your disappointment, but Sir Donald and Lady Geddes assumed that Imogen would be accompanied by you as a rule rather than me. In her absence her ladyship believed Imogen would appreciate a familiar face by her side when you are unable to bear her company."

"Serafina is the most congenial companion," Imogen was quick to add, looking eagerly at her godmother.

"I daresay. Well, seeing you are to be resident in my house for the foreseeable future, I insist you tell me all about yourself. How did you find yourself in this lamentable position?"

Serafina was slightly taken aback but recovered sufficiently to reply. "I have been working as an archivist to Sir Donald for some time. My work at

Coverdale was just coming to an end when Lady Geddes was taken ill, and it was suggested that I come up with Imogen in her stead."

Lady Wolcot nodded and then asked, "Pray tell me, what *is* an archivist?"

"Oh, Serafina is most efficient," Imogen assured her. "Papa was delighted with the work she did in his library. All our papers and books have been cataloged, for that is what the work involves, and I'm persuaded she will be only too pleased to do the same for you when she is not bearing me company."

Lady Wolcot laughed gruffly. "That is a decidedly odd occupation for a female. In any event, I have no library here, just a few books in the study for those who need to browse occasionally. My treasured collection consists of the snuffboxes you can see over there." She waved her hand toward a table where they stood. Dozens of them covered the top of a drum table, many studded with precious stones, the least valuable beautifully enameled. "They mostly belonged to my late husband, some to his father before him."

"They are very beautiful," Serafina agreed.

"And exceedingly valuable, more than the finest books, you may be sure." When she looked again at Serafina, she found the gimlet gaze most disconcerting. "Imogen will soon enough be settled—I have no doubt on that score—but what do you hope to do afterward?"

"The same as before, ma'am. I hope Sir Donald will be kind enough to furnish me with a recommendation so I may find a congenial post, similar to the one I occupied in his house."

"Serafina is determined to earn sufficient to buy her brother a commission in a good regiment."

Once again the countess raised her quizzing glass. "Indeed? And how do you hope to achieve that, may I ask?"

"By my work, ma'am. It is the only way I know."

"Very worthy, I'm sure, but how did you come to such a strange calling?"

"My father was an archivist, and I learned all I know from him."

"Is he still alive?"

"I am now, alas, an orphan and have been for some years."

"Have you no relatives?"

"My aunt is Mrs. Jonas Wyndham of Wyndham House, Coverdale."

"Ah, at last I see how you have become connected to the Geddes family."

"My aunt and Lady Geddes are neighbors and friends."

"Your aunt is evidently a generous woman to harbor two penniless orphans beneath her roof, for that is what you and your brother must be."

"My brother and I were educated through a family trust," Serafina answered, and although she kept her manner warm, she was becoming increasingly annoyed at Lady Wolcot's impudent remarks.

"You are quite a singular young lady. We do not, I must warn you, indulge in bluestocking pursuits here, so I trust you will not grow too bored when Imogen begins to go about in society."

Serafina laughed genuinely at last. "I am sure I shall not, my lady. I simply wish to be of as much assistance to Imogen as I am able, and to you, too, if you wish it, ma'am."

"There is no doubt the next few months are going to be hectic. I asked Imogen to come up to town early so that she could be furnished with the correct apparel, and I can see quite clearly it is necessary."

Imogen's initial smile faded. "Am I so outmoded, my lady?"

"Only by London standards, but have no fear, you will soon be all the crack, my dear. I have every intention of launching you into society in a splendid manner, just as your Mama would do if she were here." She glanced at Serafina then, some of the warmth going out of her manner. "When we are invited out, you understand it will not be necessary for you to accompany us."

"Naturally not, my lady."

"If we do not dine out, invariably I receive visitors here, and I think it would be proper if you would dine with the servants on those occasions." Imogen gasped as her godmother went on quickly, "Tonight you may as well remain, for the servants will already have eaten."

"Of course, my lady," Serafina replied, not at all surprised or miffed.

However, Imogen said with surprising resolve, "With the greatest respect, my lady, Serafina always lived with the family at Coverdale. Mama and Papa would not have had it any other way."

"Imogen dearest, this is Lady Wolcot's house,"

her friend reminded her in some embarrassment. "Here it must be as she wishes."

"I could not be happy if you are to be treated no better than a servant."

"It makes no odds to me I assure you." She glanced apologetically at the countess. "I do beg your pardon on Imogen's behalf, my lady."

"I really cannot countenance your being treated as a servant, Serafina," Imogen insisted, becoming even more agitated. Then looking at her godmother, she said, "I don't believe you can realize that Serafina is well connected, my lady, and that is why this error has been made. She is related to Mr. Wallace Wyndham. Mrs. Wyndham of Coverdale is his mother."

All at once the countess looked interested. "The Wyndhams of Piccadilly?"

"Wallace Wyndham is my cousin, ma'am," Serafina replied, feeling uncomfortable, for she was certain he would not like her using his name to impress.

One of Lady Wolcot's eyebrows rose a little. "With such family connections I do wonder why they don't give you a Season."

"I have no portion, ma'am, and I would not have them provide me with one, so a Season would be of no avail."

"That attitude, if I may say so, is exceedingly foolhardy." She then addressed her goddaughter again. "My dear child, if you are set upon Miss D'Arblay dining with us, then she shall and let there be an end to this tiresome matter."

Serafina began to protest, but once again Lady

Wolcot put up one hand to silence her. "Let us not broach the subject again, ladies," she insisted, and Serafina cast Imogen an angry look, but the younger girl remained unrepentant.

Before any further comment could be made on any subject, a knock on the door heralded the arrival of one of the footmen.

"Mr. Stanway has arrived, my lady."

Quite a remarkable change came over the countess at that moment. Her smile widened, and she began to look coy.

"Don't delay, my man. Show him in immediately." Then she turned excitedly to Imogen. "Mr. Stanway is a great friend of mine, my dear, and I cannot wait for you to make his acquaintance. You are bound to find him as diverting as I do."

A moment later the footman ushered in Foster Stanway, and both young ladies stared at him in astonishment. He wasn't very tall, but his demeanor could only be described as exquisite. It was evident his hair had been teased and pomaded into the style known as *à la Titus*, his shirt collar almost touched his ears, his neck cloth was folded in the manner called *à la Americain*, and the width of his evening coat could not possibly be accounted for by the mere breadth of his shoulders alone.

"Come in, come in, dear boy," Lady Wolcot urged, and she sat forward in her chair. "I would have you meet my goddaughter, who I have often mentioned to you and who has only just arrived in town."

He minced across the room, taking the countess's hand and raising it to his rouged lips. "As always you look amazing, my dear," he lisped. "Quite, quite amazing."

"Flatterer," she responded, looking nonetheless delighted. "My goddaughter is going to create quite a sensation when she makes her debut. Is she not a dear, Fos?"

Foster Stanway turned on his heel and raising his quizzing glass from among an assortment of fobs and seals dangling from his waist, he inspected the two young ladies at length.

"Good grief! What an exquisite vision," he declared at last, "but do tell, my lady, which beauty is Miss Geddes?"

Imogen sniggered foolishly, while Serafina smiled wryly. She stood to one side as her young friend sketched a curtsy.

"I am Imogen Geddes," she said shyly.

"I declare that London is about to be transformed by the addition of one so lovely."

He glanced curiously at Serafina, and then Lady Wolcot explained in a disapproving tone, "Miss D'Arblay has come as companion to my goddaughter, Fos."

The young man laughed. "La! A companion indeed. All those I have encountered before have usually been herring-gutted old cats. What a pleasant change. You could set a new standard in paid companions."

"You are very kind to say so, sir," Serafina responded, and it was evident he was unaware of her sarcasm.

Foster Stanway continued to gaze at her admiringly. "Well, you may be certain *I* shall not call you a dirty dish."

"Imogen," Lady Wolcot said sharply making the girl start, "there will be a large number of other girls coming out next Season, so I urge you when a gentleman addresses you to stand forward, otherwise others will shine in your stead."

At so direct a barb, Serafina made a mental note to stay well in the background in the future, which, in any event, would suit her very well indeed. A moment later, Lady Wolcot claimed Mr. Stanway's attention, which coincided with the arrival of several more guests. The females were all of a similar age to Lady Wolcot, and the gentlemen inclined to be foppish in their mode of dress. All of them showed a very great interest in the newcomers, especially Serafina. It was as if her poverty and need to earn a living was a great curiosity to them.

At dinner Lady Wolcot sat with Foster Stanway at one side of her and Imogen, looking bewildered, on her other side. Serafina, seated at the far end of the table, well below the salt, joined in the conversation whenever she could, but it was often about people of whom she had no knowledge, so she contented herself by listening to every *on-dit.*

Food was plentiful; fish, meat, and fowl, and everyone present availed themselves of it freely. Wine was similarly free flowing, with glasses being filled as soon as they became half-empty. Very soon most of the guests were decidedly bosky.

"Cut up a great lark last night, didn't we, Fos?" Sir Walter Edgecombe called across the table.

"It was a bit of a rumption, I own," Mr. Stanway replied, laughing at the memory.

"What *were* you gentlemen about?" Lady Wolcot asked, looking curious as she gnawed voraciously on a large chicken leg.

"It wasn't anything out of the ordinary," the young man assured her, laughing again.

The other guests urged him to tell, and Lady Wolcot said, "It was either a great lark or it wasn't."

"We came across a Charley in his box at Temple Bar," he explained, sipping his wine and almost spilling it in the process. "Well, being a trifle bosky . . . we just tipped up the box and left the wretched fellow facedown in the road trapped under it!"

The revelation caused a great ripple of laughter around the table, although Serafina could not see what was so amusing about abusing an officer of the watch so thoroughly.

"What scaff and raff you are to be sure," Lady Wolcot clucked, but looked not in the least annoyed by their childish antics. "You're all past praying for."

"The fellow still contrived to shake his rattle, even though he was trapped," Sir Walter added, almost choking with laughter as he continued to eat, "so foxed or not, we decided to hop the twig before we were caught."

"What could they have done to us if we had been caught?" Mr. Stanway demanded. "The answer in short, is nothing!"

"I wonder if he has been freed yet?" Sir Walter asked, laughing uproariously again.

By the time the puddings and syllabubs were placed upon the table and immediately fallen upon by the other guests, Serafina wished Lady Wolcot's order for her to eat in the servant's quarters still stood, for she was quite certain their manner of eating must be rather more civilized.

When, at last, the interminable meal was finished, the ladies adjourned to the drawing room for coffee while the gentlemen remained in the dining room to take their port.

"Fos is always so diverting," Lady Wolcot confided to one of her guests as they walked back into the drawing room.

"And so devoted to you, dearest."

"We shall all be obliged to put on our thinking caps," one lady commented coyly as Serafina handed around the cups of coffee, "and compile a list of eligible young men for Miss Geddes's consideration."

The girl's cheeks grew pink as her godmother replied in a derisory manner, "You may rest assured, my dear Mrs. Webb, that I have been engaged in such a task for several weeks past."

"I should have known you would be up to the rigs in this matter," answered the chastened Mrs. Webb.

"Young Pendleton is exceedingly handsome," one lady suggested, "and he's been on the catch for a wife for a few Seasons."

"A possibility," Lady Wolcot mused as she sipped at her coffee thoughtfully. "Yes, he is certainly eligible."

"If that is so, why has he not yet settled?" Imogen asked.

"He's hanging out for a fortune, my dear," Mrs. Resco told her.

Imogen sank back into the cushions of the sofa. "Oh . . ." she murmured.

Serafina cast her a sympathetic look, but Imogen continued to appear dismayed, and her friend could not help but pity her just then. There were, she reflected, definite advantages in being poor, but she didn't suppose anyone present in the room would agree with her upon that point.

"You will never guess what I was told today," Mrs. Webb announced, looking excited.

"No, I don't suppose we shall," Lady Wolcot chided.

"Amy Cranham heard it from Lily Wilby, who is a bosom friend of none other than Mirabel Betteridge . . ."

"Another *on-dit* about her brother, Trenton, I do not doubt," Mrs. Resco replied, looking bored. "Not a sennight passes by without an *on-dit* about Trenton circulating. If he raises one finger, it is talked about endlessly. I confess, I do not care if his lordship wears a buff coat or a blue one, or indeed if he has four horses drawing his curricle rather than the usual two."

When the woman had finished, Mrs. Webb said triumphantly, "Amy Cranham declares that he's at last on the catch for a wife!"

The statement had a strange effect upon the others in the room. All heads snapped up, turban feathers vibrating. Then Lady Wolcot laughed derisively. "What humbug! If ever there was a confirmed bachelor, Trenton is he. Who told Mrs.

Cranham that cawker? He'll never put himself into the parson's mousetrap."

"Who can know better than his own sister?" the woman insisted.

"*If* it is she who has said so," Lady Wolcot said, "I am persuaded it cannot be, for Mirabel Betteridge is no tattle-basket."

"Well, Amy Cranham vows she heard it from Lily Wilby, who is very close to her ladyship."

"If it is true, there is no bigger catch," the countess mused, glancing at Imogen in a calculating manner.

"Don't you consider he's a trifle *old* for Miss Geddes?" Mrs. Resco ventured.

The countess laughed derisively. "You may be sure Viscount Trenton will not be seeking a bride from among the spinsters and widows who throng the drawing rooms of the *ton*, although I own sufficient numbers of them toady around him whenever he ventures forth. Oh no, you may be certain if he is seeking to fix his interest, he will look to the ranks of debutantes. Mark my words, ladies."

At this point the gentlemen joined them. Having imbibed freely of the port, their spirits were certainly as high as their coloring.

"Have *you* heard the tattle that Lord Trenton is hanging out for a bride?" Lady Wolcot asked of Mr. Stanway.

His answer was an immediate laugh. "If that is so, we should all give prodigious thanks."

"Oh? Why are you so concerned for his marital status?" the countess asked, looking suspicious.

"Are you, by any chance, rivals for the same cyprian?"

"I would not look in the same direction, I assure you, for every other female I encounter pales beside you, my dear," he vowed, and the countess looked foolishly pleased by his flummery. "However, should Trenton become leg-shackled, a young wife would undoubtedly keep him at home, allowing some of us to game without invariably losing our purses. He has the most amazing luck at the tables."

"I doubt if marriage would keep Trenton away from the tables, or indeed his cyprian," Sir Walter chided. "And while we are speaking of such matters, I believe it is time to chance the dice."

"In your condition you won't even be able to see the spots," his friend told him laughingly.

Footmen were setting up tables, and most of the guests were displaying great eagerness to begin gambling.

"Come along, Miss Geddes," Foster Stanway invited, "allow me to show you how to throw dice."

"I have only ever played whist," she protested.

Some of the others laughed. "You will soon learn other more exciting ways to chance your money," Sir Walter assured her.

Serafina was glad enough to be able to retire to a quiet corner with her sewing while the others set about playing faro and hazard with a vengeance. From time to time she glanced worriedly at Imogen, who appeared flushed and was enjoying the unfamiliar games. Lots of noise emanated from the tables as someone won or lost.

After a while Foster Stanway strolled up to her, taking a pinch of snuff. "Why do you not join us, Miss D'Arblay? Dame Fortune often favors beginners."

"I do not—cannot—gamble, sir. I have no resources, you see."

"If only those of us who are solvent gambled, ma'am, precious few would be able to do so."

"My vowels would be useless."

He laughed. "That is only supposing you lose. Come now, you must have some pin money."

"What I have I must needs keep by me."

"Remarkable," he murmured, and when, a moment later, Lady Wolcot called him, he smiled philosophically and went to join her.

When Serafina finally took her leave of the party, she knew she would not be missed, and as cheerless as her room was, she was glad to reach it.

Lying in the narrow bed, she felt quite strongly that Sir Donald and Lady Geddes would not much like the circle in which their daughter's godmother moved.

# FOUR

When Imogen and Serafina finally came out of the rather dark interior of Harding Howells, the linen-drapers in Pall Mall, they blinked in the bright sunlight of the day.

For some considerable time they had agonized over the most exquisite bolts of cloth. Was blue-striped poplin more becoming than puce sarcenet? Or pink satin more favored than gold brocade? Imogen had arrived in London with a carte blanche from her parents to enable her to dress herself grandly, and therefore discussions as to what she should purchase were endless.

To the surprise and pleasure of both young ladies, Lady Wolcot had forsaken her duty and airily instructed Serafina to accompany Imogen on all her shopping excursions for the time being, commenting that she may as well earn the generous salary Sir Donald was paying her.

Personally Serafina thought Imogen needed more expert guidance on what best to choose, but both young ladies had studied well *La Belle Assemblée* of late and knew instinctively what was right to choose from all that was offered to them by eager tradesmen.

Lengths of Indian cotton, the finest sprigged muslin, glossy satins, fine tulles and lustrings were at last purchased and placed in Lady Wolcot's carriage, which had been put at their disposal.

"I had no notion how tiring shopping could be!" Serafina declared as she gratefully climbed into the carriage. "Nor did I expect the choice to be so great."

Imogen chuckled. "It certainly beats the choice we had in Winchester. My feet ache so much, and yet I have found this morning a delightful experience. Such beautiful materials. I loved the striped poplin, and even now wonder if I should have purchased a length of that, too, but no, I declare I have enough to occupy Lady Wolcot's mantua maker for quite some time to come."

Serafina laughed wryly as the carriage set off. "There is no doubt of *that*!"

Imogen peered out of the window, bright-eyed. "Have you noticed how very modish everyone is here in London?"

"In truth I had not."

"It's just like looking at one fashion plate after the other. Coachman, take us to Bond Street if you please."

Her friend groaned good-naturedly. "Can we not save Bond Street for another day, Imogen? I am quite exhausted."

"No, indeed, we cannot. I am enjoying myself hugely, and so, I'm persuaded, are you."

Serafina could not deny the fact. Indeed, tired as

she was, it was preferable to returning to Wolcot House, where she felt less than welcome. It seemed obvious that Lady Wolcot had, for some reason, taken her in dislike, although she was happy enough for Serafina to accompany Imogen everywhere so that she, the countess, was able to go about her own business, whatever that might be.

If Serafina was to be honest, she could not summon up any real liking for Lady Wolcot, who seemed, despite her elevated position, a trifle coarse. Nor did she have much affection for Lady Wolcot's cronies, who were of a similar ilk. From all she had so far observed, they drank too deep and gamed until their pockets were to let.

Foster Stanway was a frequent visitor to Wolcot House and appeared to be on intimate terms with the countess, despite the fact he was several years younger; but that did not prevent him looking appreciatively at Imogen and Serafina whenever he believed her ladyship was not aware of it. On consideration, Serafina was definitely in no desperate hurry to return to Wolcot House any sooner than was absolutely necessary.

The carriage came to a halt outside James Smyth's perfumery shop in Bond Street, and its two passengers alighted. The perfumery was a delightful place, and the two young ladies browsed there happily for some time before Imogen bought some eau de cologne, and Serafina purchased a supply of much needed red pomatum for her lips.

From Mr. Smyth's perfumery shop they moved on to peer into Mr. Robinson's confectionery shop with its delicious array of sweetmeats that tempted all who passed by. Imogen just could not resist buying some comfits, and both girls were laughing merrily when they came out of the shop a short time later.

"Serafina, do you consider that Mr. Stanway is Lady Wolcot's . . . cicisbeo?"

Serafina cast her friend a wry look. "I think it is very likely, don't you?"

Imogen began to laugh again. "At least he isn't like Sir Walter Edgecombe. How fat he is! He wears a corset that creaks every time he moves and almost sends me into whoops. Have you noticed?"

"How could I not? I also noted that he contrives to eat everything in sight! I was obliged to hide my napkin the other evening for fear he would eat that, too!"

Imogen laughed merrily before she said, "I was amazed at how much money crossed the tables the other evening, and I heard say that at White's and Boodles' some of the stakes can be enormous. All Lady Wolcot's acquaintances game exceedingly deep I noticed."

"I do trust you will not get into the habit of gaming deep, Imogen," Serafina told her, suddenly serious.

The girl sighed. "Everyone I have met so far seems to be addicted to gaming, but I lost several guineas the other evening, so I decided then I was not lucky in games of chance."

"No one is—at least not for long," Serafina pointed out, feeling somewhat relieved.

"Mr. Stanway said I must persist, that my luck

would change eventually, but in all truth, Serafina, I found it quite tedious after a while."

Imogen looked up and down the street. Many carriages awaited their passengers at the curbside, and the girl began to look somewhat puzzled. "I wonder where Lady Wolcot's carriage can be. They all look alike to me, and there are so many of them!"

Serafina joined her search, but then she stiffened somewhat when her gaze took in what appeared to be an all too familiar curricle. Belatedly she realized there were several similar equipages in the area, and she relaxed again, feeling a little foolish. Until that moment she had thought that unpleasant and disturbing incident was gone from her memory.

"There it is!" Imogen cried triumphantly, catching sight of the carriage and its attendant footman.

It seemed strange to Serafina to go about so well accompanied. In the country, Imogen had been allowed abroad with only Serafina for company, and Serafina herself rode alone whenever she stayed at her aunt's house.

"Serafina! Miss Geddes!"

Just as they started toward the carriage, at the sound of their names being called, both young ladies turned around. Serafina's eyes opened wide with surprise to see her cousin's wife hurrying toward them, a page scampering behind her in an effort to keep up.

"Caroline! What a surprise it is to see you."

The young woman's expression was one of curiosity. "No more than it is to see *you*. What are you doing in London?"

"I am to come out next Season," Imogen explained pertly, "and Serafina is acting as my companion while we are staying at my godmother's house."

"Your godmother? Am I acquainted with the lady?"

"Lady Wolcot is very prominent in society. I'm persuaded you must be acquainted with her."

Caroline Wyndham nodded wryly. "Oh, yes indeed. Wallace's mama is very remiss in not telling us you were coming up to London, so you must forgive my surprise. No doubt she will tell us all about it in her next communication. Wallace will be surprised when I tell him of our meeting. He's in Gentleman Jackson's Saloon at the moment." She glanced across the road to a building on the other side. "Fighting with one's fists is quite a craze among gentlemen at present. The great Gentleman Jackson is amassing a fortune teaching them to fight. Wallace is quite proud of his prowess. Well, how exciting it must be for you, Imogen."

"I confess to be enjoying myself hugely, ma'am," the girl admitted. "Of course, the Season is not yet begun, when I expect to be enjoying myself even more! I have just purchased materials to make some of my new clothes."

"I do trust you left a little for me!"

Imogen looked rueful. "Just a little, ma'am, until the next consignment."

Caroline Wyndham turned to Serafina then. "What a splendid opportunity this is for you, my dear. Mayhap you will be fortunate enough to spend your time well and find yourself a congenial match when the Season begins."

Serafina laughed, and Imogen said, "I have made a similar wish, Mrs. Wyndham."

"How opportune it is that we have met today, for I am holding a soiree in the very near future. Although I am bound to confess Lady Wolcot is not usually on my guest list, you may be certain you all will be on this occasion. I must dash away now. I always take tea with the children, you see. Until then . . ."

With a wave of her hand she hurried away, followed by her page. The two young ladies watched as she climbed into her carriage, which immediately set off in the direction of Piccadilly where Wallace Wyndham had his palatial home. Serafina had heard much talk of it while residing at her aunt's house, and she wondered now if it was as fine as Lady Wolcot's.

"What a dear she is," Imogen mused, a smile remaining on her lips as they waved to the departing carriage.

"When Wallace and Caroline became betrothed, we all wondered how he had contrived to make a match with someone so delightful."

Imogen chuckled knowingly. "He is rather starched, not to mention toplofty."

"He was an unbearable little boy," Serafina recalled, "and I am afraid he is still a considerable snob."

After Caroline had gone, Imogen climbed into the carriage; just as Serafina was about to follow, she happened to glance across the road, and her eyes opened wide to find herself staring at a very familiar face. Wearing a buff driving coat with countless capes and fastened with mother-of-pearl buttons was the man she had encountered on her arrival in London. He had just been about to take the ribbons of his curricle from his tiger, and from the surprise on his face, he was equally shocked to see her.

A moment later she hurried into the carriage and sat down beside Imogen, who was totally unaware of her friend's surprise.

"I believe we should leave Nickolay's Fur and Feather Manufactury until another day," the girl decided, and Serafina nodded her agreement.

As the carriage set off, she saw as she glanced obliquely through the window that the man was now in conversation with an acquaintance and oblivious to her. Serafina felt quite shaken to have encountered him again, but could not understand why the sight of one insolent buck should have discomposed her so.

Imogen was chattering on about her plans for the various materials she had purchased. Madam Arcadia, the renowned mantua maker, was calling at Wolcot House to discuss designs for Imogen's new wardrobe of clothes. Serafina contrived well enough to converse with her on the subject, although her mind was not fully attentive on this occasion.

As Lady Wolcot's carriage moved away from the curb, the young man who had caused Serafina so much consternation had been about to climb onto the box of his curricle, but now he turned to an acquaintance who had followed him out of Gentleman Jackson's Saloon.

"Fossdyke, who was that dashing creature who just got into the laudalet? Do you, by any chance, know her?"

Mr. Fossdyke raised his quizzing glass in the direction of the departing carriage before answering in an indolent manner, "That's the Wolcot carriage, so I suppose it is safe to assume she's the chit who Lady Wolcot is about to bring out. A ward or goddaughter, or some such thing. At least that is what all the prattle-boxes are saying."

The other man looked amused and slightly disbelieving. "Lady Wolcot? That mantrap?"

"The chit has a fair fortune, I'm told, as well as being a beauty, as you have obviously noted." Mr. Fossdyke smiled slyly then. "Don't tell me you're interested in a green girl just out of the schoolroom. Well, if that don't beat the Dutch!"

The other man shrugged his broad shoulders and bestowed upon him a charming smile. "You know me rather better than that, don't you? It's just my natural curiosity. I like to know what's going on in town just as much as the old tabbies."

"I didn't believe for one moment you were likely to give up the delightful Corinna for that green girl." Mr. Fossdyke smiled again. "Not that I would mind if you did. More chance for me! See you at Five's Court on the morrow, eh? Morris fights the Dancer. Last time Morris knocked him into horse nails after that nozzler. It will be a mill to watch and no mistake!"

His friend looked thoughtful as he nodded and then climbed up onto the box at last, flicked his

room. "It is in my reticule," Lady Wolcot told them, a note of irritation creeping into her voice.

It was Serafina who located it and administered it to the countess, who immediately began to revive.

"What ails you, my lady?" Imogen asked, casting a worried look at her godmother. "Are you laced too tightly perchance?"

"Tush!" was Lady Wolcot's uncompromising reply. "What nonsense you speak! I shall be quite recovered in a moment. It was just the shock of realization that brought on one of my spasms, which I regret to say are all too frequent of late."

"The realization of what, my lady?" the girl insisted, looking puzzled now.

The countess took in a deep breath, pushed away the vinaigrette, and sat up again, brandishing an engraved invitation. "Lady Betteridge is Lord Trenton's sister, and we are invited to her rout. That, to me, is quite significant."

Once again Serafina and Imogen exchanged baffled looks. "Oh, what goosecaps you are to be sure! Lord Trenton is the greatest catch of all," the countess gasped. "Mayhap she wishes to inspect all the new debutantes in the event . . ."

Imogen looked disgusted. "You make me sound like a piece of horseflesh, my lady, and I don't care for that."

Lady Wolcot laughed. "My dear, the marriage market operates in a very similar manner to that at Tattersalls."

"Oh, I cannot credit that!" cried the shocked girl, and Serafina wished the countess could couch her statements in a more diplomatic manner than she had so far exhibited.

"Young bucks make bids for the best horses at Tattersalls. At Almack's and in the drawing rooms of the *ton*, it is females who catch the eye. It is a system that works well enough whether horses are wanted or wives, and talking of Almack's, Lady Betteridge may well be our passport to vouchers. She is a crony of Countess Lieven, one of the patronesses."

Imogen continued to look dismayed as Lady Wolcot became agitated once more. "Tell me, child, are any of your new gowns nearing completion?"

"I believe so, my lady. Madam Arcadia did say they would be ready by Wednesday, except for one pelisse, and that is only because I have been tardy in obtaining the frogging and epaulets from Swan and Edgar."

"That is of no account. What matters is that you will be ready to face the world beautifully gowned as befits my goddaughter. No one will be able to say I did not bring you out in anything but the most magnificent manner. I tell you, child, most alliances are contracted *before* the Season begins, and I beg you to bear that in mind at all times. There is no reason why you should not make a very elevated match." Lady Wolcot stared down at the coveted invitation and frowned. "How odd it is that your name, Miss D'Arblay, is also included. I can understand your being invited to the Wyndhams' hurricane, but this is most perplexing, I own. . . ."

Serafina started visibly at the mention of her own

name. "How can that be?" she asked. "No one aside from yourself and Mrs. Wyndham knows that I am in town."

Lady Wolcot's brow suddenly cleared. "Mayhap it was Mrs. Wyndham who has mentioned your name to her ladyship. Yes, that is what it is, you may be sure. They are, after all, close neighbors, and one cannot blame her for trying to put forward your name whenever possible."

"There is no possible reason for me to attend Lady Betteridge's rout," Serafina answered, feeling that the disclaimer was expected of her.

In any event she had no wish to go.

"You must go!" Imogen insisted, looking outraged. "Oh, do tell her she must, my lady! I shall enjoy it so much more if Serafina is there, too."

The countess drew yet another sigh. "I fear Imogen is correct, Miss D'Arblay. You must go. On this occasion you will be obliged to put your own wishes to one side. If this is Mrs. Wyndham's doing, we must not offend her. We must contrive to offend no one in Imogen's come-out year, lest it reflects badly upon her."

She lumbered to her feet and made to go to the door, hesitating for a moment when she was halfway across the room. "Oh, Miss D'Arblay, I had almost forgotten in my excitement, but there is a letter for you."

She handed it to Serafina, who immediately recognized her brother's hand. When Lady Wolcot had gone, she retreated to a chair to read it, while Imogen returned to the pianoforte and picked at the keys in a disconsolate manner.

"Now Lady Wolcot has given me this news, splendid as it is I do not doubt, I am all of a twitter. These diversions are all very toplofty affairs, I fancy. How can I concentrate on the pianoforte when I am wondering about making my debut in society so early. I didn't believe I would be obliged to attend any formal functions until after I had made my debut. I'm not nearly ready."

"Just think of it as a soiree at home at Coverdale," Serafina suggested. "It won't be much different."

"Except for the *ton*, and who *is* this Lord Trenton Lady Wolcot keeps mentioning?"

Serafina shook her head. "I have no more notion than you, but I have no doubt we shall know on Thursday if he attends Caroline's soiree. If not, we may be obliged to wait until his sister's rout."

"The way everyone was talking about him the other evening, he sounded ancient. I hope he doesn't look like Sir Walter Edgecombe—a gouty old brandy face!"

Serafina burst out laughing. "Oh surely not! Even Lady Wolcot would not consider him a fitting match for you, dearest."

"Do not be so sure. All anyone seems to care about is my marrying someone with a great fortune and position. If he's fat and has warts all over his face, that won't matter in the least."

Despite having made light of her friend's fears, Serafina understood them all too well and gave her a considered look. "Imogen, remember you are not obliged to marry, or even receive the attentions of anyone you do not like."

"I have not, as yet, met anyone I can vaguely like, certainly not Mr. Stanway or Sir Walter, who Lady Wolcot considers diverting company. I am bound to confess if everyone in the beau monde is of the same ilk, I feel certain I shall not meet a suitable match and eventually return home a spinster."

"Don't despair, dearest. It is early days as yet, so don't seek to judge everyone by Lady Wolcot's acquaintances. You are bound to encounter some very presentable young men before long."

"I daresay you are correct," Imogen replied, but with no enthusiasm evident in her manner.

"At this time of the year many of them will be out of town, at Brighton or at their hunting boxes in the country. You will see, everything will change once the Season has begun. Why don't you practice the pianoforte in the event you are asked to play at some function?"

As Imogen picked out a desultory tune on the instrument, Serafina quickly read Jolyon's letter. As she had expected, it was not a newsy note of what was happening in Coverdale, more a number of questions relating to Imogen. As she put it away in her pocket, she did not look forward to answering, for she could give him no real hope.

Just as she put the letter away, Imogen finished her playing on a discordant note and got to her feet. "Is that a letter from Jolyon?"

"Yes."

"I thought it must be. Why did he not write to me?"

"I daresay he considered it unwise under the circumstances."

The girl attempted to affect a careless attitude as she asked, "Did he mention me at all?'

"He mentioned no one else."

The girl wrung her hands together in anguish. "I wish he were here," she said and then rushed out of the room before Serafina could stop her.

# FIVE

Despite her worries, Imogen looked startlingly beautiful when dressed in one of her new evening gowns. The simply styled yellow muslin with gold spangles suited her to perfection. The narrow gold fillet in her hair was all that was needed to complete the outfit.

Lady Wolcot indicated her approval and looked satisfied also when she viewed Serafina's dowdy velvet. Serafina did not mind in the least the dowdiness of her own clothes; they were entirely in keeping with her position, but she was certain her cousin, Wallace Wyndham, would not take kindly to seeing so poor a relative in the salons of the haut monde.

As usual Lady Wolcot was overdressed in a silver-spangled muslin gown that was both too young in style and too tight for her ample curves. Diamonds adorned much of her visible flesh, of which there was plenty.

Imogen's cheeks were pink with excitement as Lady Wolcot instructed, "Remember to smile as often as you can, dear. If a gentleman bores you with his conversation, you must not show it on any account. You must contrive to be pleasant to everyone, even if you do not find them amiable. You have no notion who is influential and who is not."

"I will contrive to remember all you have said," Imogen vowed, but she was scarcely able to suppress her excitement.

It appeared to Serafina that her concern at being married off to some elderly rake had disappeared.

Just as the carriage that would take them to the Wyndhams' house came to a halt outside, Foster Stanway strolled in.

"Why, I can see I am just in time to find you at home," he greeted them. "What utter visions of loveliness you all are."

"We are going to a soiree at Wyndham House," Lady Wolcot announced importantly, and it suddenly occurred to Serafina that the countess was not often invited to the very best *ton* parties, something that was quite a revelation.

Far from doing Imogen a service in bringing her out into society, it appeared that her godchild's presence was going to elevate Lady Wolcot from her usual rackety cronies to much more refined company. Serafina could not help but smile at the irony of the situation.

Mr. Stanway's eyebrows rose slightly. "You are mixing in elevated circles nowadays, my dear."

"Are you intimating that I normally do not?" the countess asked in an outraged tone.

Not in the least taken aback, he laughed as he slowly walked around each lady in turn, inspecting them closely, much to Serafina's discomfort.

"I believe you are like to be moving in even higher company before much longer."

"What do you mean by that, Fos?" the countess asked, evidently intrigued by his cryptic remark.

"I joined Fossdyke over dinner at Watiers' earlier this evening. He has excellent taste in wine. Are you by any chance acquainted with the fellow?"

"Yes, yes, naturally I am," the countess responded irritably.

"He divulged, in his cups, that he had been conversing with Trenton in Bond Street the other day and he—Trenton that is—was expressing a good deal of curiosity about Miss Geddes."

Imogen started, her eyes becoming wide. "Surely he cannot know me."

"Evidently he must have caught sight of you and was sufficiently impressed to ask who you were."

Lady Wolcot looked triumphant. "I knew it! How splendid that news is to me."

"I knew it would be," the young man replied, looking smug as he took a pinch of snuff.

"What a triumph that would be. Imogen and Viscount Trenton."

"Mayhap I should wager upon the outcome in the book at White's," Mr. Stanway suggested.

"Don't you dare!" the countess exclaimed, losing none of the good spirits with which his news had endowed her. "Nothing must spoil the natural progression of any courtship, Fos."

"It appears I am going to be deprived of your company today," he went on. "The least you could do, after bearing you this splendid news, is afford me a little of your renowned hospitality."

"Help yourself," Lady Wolcot told him, waving her hand in the air. It was evident her thoughts were dwelling upon his astounding news. "We must go with no further ado."

He bowed toward them as he helped each lady into the carriage, and then he hurried back into the house to avail himself of Lady Wolcot's hospitality with no further delay.

Serafina's cousin's house was larger than she had expected it to be, with a semicircular carriage drive bordered by iron railings and a porte cochere under which the carriages stopped to discharge their passengers. Lamps illuminated the outside of the mansion, and countless candles lit up every room, endowing it with an inviting air. Although it was Serafina's cousin's establishment, it could have been anyone's as far as she was concerned, for the rooms were crowded with people, none of whom she knew.

It had taken some considerable time for the carriage to make its way along Piccadilly and let them down beneath the porte cochere, due to the very many other carriages making their way to Wyndham House.

As soon as they arrived, Lady Wolcot took hold of Imogen's arm and led her away to be introduced to a number of important people, making it absolutely clear that Serafina was to be left to her own devices. As she looked around, every face was a strange one. Fortunately very soon after her arrival, Caroline sought her out.

"I'm so glad you were able to come," she told Serafina, and her sincerity could not be doubted.

"This is my very first *ton* party, Caroline. Nothing was ever so grand as this in Coverdale, and I am bound to confess I find it a trifle overwhelming."

"If one holds a diversion, it is politic to invite as many guests as possible. This type of function is always a squeeze."

"How are the children? They must be growing fast. It's so long since I saw them."

"You must come around for tea one day. I assure you, you will be glad to go back to Lady Wolcot's house. By the by, how do you like staying with her?"

Serafina looked wry. "It is comfortable, and in any event I am only resident there until Imogen is settled."

"Looking as she does tonight, I don't believe that will take very long. Of course," she added wryly, "Lady Wolcot is something of a drawback to any girl's aspirations."

"Oh, I'm persuaded she means well."

"Does she still have Foster Stanway as a gallant?"

"Yes, indeed. She appears to be devoted to him, although Imogen and I cannot conceive why."

"Oh dear, what a man-milliner he is. Wallace cannot abide the fellow. Serafina, do go along to the ballroom and have some champagne. The dancing will begin soon, and as always you will wish to participate. At Coverdale we can never keep you off the dance floor."

"In Coverdale I know everyone!"

"You will contrive, I have no doubt. Wallace is around somewhere, and I know he will be anxious to have words with you, and you may be certain I will endeavor to present you to as many people as possible."

"Don't trouble yourself on my behalf, Caroline, I beg of you. I can see you have a rather hectic evening ahead of you." As a portly gentleman with a florid complexion attempted, with great difficulty, to squeeze past them, Serafina suddenly frowned. "Caroline, do you know a Lord Trenton by any chance?"

The woman's eyes rolled back in their sockets. "Who does not? Why do you ask?"

"Lady Wolcot believes he would make a good match for Imogen. What do you think?"

Caroline choked back her laughter. "Unless I am very much mistaken, Robert Trenton does not have a penchant for green girls, but you may be certain he *is* very eligible, and Imogen is very lovely."

"That, at least, is some comfort."

Caroline Wyndham frowned suddenly. "Weren't Jolyon and Imogen very close when she was at home?"

Serafina drew a sigh and nodded her head. "Imogen will soon forget him after a few dazzling evenings like this one and a deal of flattery, but for my poor brother it will not be so easy. He is head over ears in love with her."

"How unfair life can be," Caroline mused, considering Serafina thoughtfully before she moved on to speak to more of her guests.

Serafina had only just reached the top of the stairs when she came face-to-face with her cousin, Wallace Wyndham. When he detached himself from a group of acquaintances, his demeanor displayed nothing of the kind of welcome afforded her by his wife.

"Serafina." He greeted her in the supercilious manner she recalled very well. "Caroline told me you were in town. I was never more surprised to hear anything."

"I have, in fact, been here for some time now," she responded, feeling all at once despondent.

"We certainly didn't look to see you here."

"As you well know, I am obliged to go where suitable employment takes me. Mayhap, on the next occasion you will be saved embarrassment, and I'll go to the country. I do prefer it in any event."

He laughed, and she was gratified to have caused him some feeling of discomposure. "Embarrassed? That is nonsense, and you know it. It distresses me to see you in such a lowly situation, that is all. Lady Wolcot of all people."

"I am employed by Sir Donald Geddes, which may afford you less discomfort."

"Whoever employs you, my dear, I don't consider you suited in the least to being a paid companion."

She cast him a look of surprise, his manner never failing to raise her anger. "What am I suited to, Wallace?" When he didn't answer, she said, "Mayhap I would be better suited to running a house like this, and giving routs and soirees." She smiled then. "I am a realist enough to know that is not possible, so I do what I can to earn my way. I promise you I will not boast of our connection, if that is what you fear."

His cheeks grew somewhat red. "You are talking such humbug, Serafina. You never used to fly up into the boughs so easily before." He glanced past her and said with evident relief, "You must excuse me for the moment; there is someone just arrived who I am obliged to greet."

As she wandered in the direction of the ballroom, Serafina immediately regretted her waspishness. However, her cousin had always, since childhood, brought out the worst in her nature, and she doubted if that would ever change.

A champagne fountain had been set up in the flower-festooned ballroom. It was already very hot in there as well as crowded, and of course no windows could be opened in the event someone might contract a chill, which seemed to be the most dreaded fear among most people she had encountered since her arrival in London.

The champagne fountain was very well attended, and Serafina helped herself to a glass and spoke briefly to various people who addressed her. After a while she went to sit in a corner where several chaperons were already ensconced.

When the music struck up, Serafina was glad to see Imogen dancing with a pleasant-looking young man. As the evening progressed, Imogen continued to be partnered by various young gentlemen who looked perfectly presentable. This was a considerable relief to Serafina, who believed there was a real fear that Lady Wolcot might try to marry Imogen off to some elderly rake if his fortune and standing was great enough.

Serafina did not in the least mind sitting in the corner with a, mainly, elderly group of chaperons. As it was the very first soiree she had ever attended in London, she found it vastly diverting. Those small parties that took place in the country could not compare. They were nowhere near as crowded, and certainly not as modish.

Serafina was dazzled by the magnificent jewelry worn by most of the ladies, and she couldn't help but admire their stylish gowns. It was a great pity Jolyon had no interest in such matters, for she could store the information to relate to him in the letters he had insisted she write to him at frequent intervals. However, she would write and relate all she had observed to Lady Geddes, for she was convinced Imogen would neglect to do so.

In the midst of the crowds she caught sight of Imogen once again, looking flushed and bright-eyed. At her side Lady Wolcot's ample bosom was swelled out more than was usual, and the smile on her face looked more than a little ingratiating. Serafina's interest quickened.

They were, she noticed then, conversing with a gentleman dressed in a dark blue evening coat that appeared to require no padding, unlike those of many of the gentlemen present, including her own cousin whose skintight breeches were abominably wrinkled. It was only when the gentleman moved to allow someone past that Serafina saw that he was none other than her old adversary from the curricle, and she began to suffer something akin to panic.

Naturally on either occasion he had not seen Imogen in her company, so he was not likely to know of any connection, which she reckoned was most fortunate. Automatically she put her fan up in front of her face just as the man said something to make Imogen and her godmother laugh.

A moment later, when a cotillion was announced, he led Imogen into the set. For some reason Serafina found her heart was beating fast. She turned quickly to the lady sitting beside her who, having attended countless other similar diversions, was now intent upon her sewing.

"Do you know the gentleman who is standing up with Miss Geddes, ma'am?"

The woman squinted myopically into the crowds. "Who?"

Serafina swallowed noisily and tried to check her impatience. "I refer to the elegant gentleman who is dancing with the lady in the yellow-spangled muslin."

The woman's lips relaxed into a smile. "Oh yes, I see them now. Why, that is Lord Trenton."

Once again Serafina stiffened, and she didn't doubt her shock was clearly etched upon her features. "Oh no, he cannot possibly be Lord Trenton."

"I assure you he is," replied the woman, casting her a curious look.

It was then that Serafina turned to her in a conciliatory manner. "I do beg your pardon, ma'am. I am acting like a peagoose. I . . . merely thought that particular gentleman was someone else. It is my mistake. I see it now."

Throughout the cotillion Serafina continued to watch them covertly over her open fan. Imogen seemed happy enough and her smile a genuine one. Lord Trenton was, she observed, a surefooted dancer. In any event he certainly was not the aging roué she had feared he might be, but he was scarcely better. From her own encounter with him, Serafina did not consider him suited in the least to a naive debutante like Imogen, and yet it was evident he was being put forward as a prime suitor. Worse, it was becoming apparent he was more than a little interested in Imogen. The knowledge of what might be to come caused her to shiver.

"Oh, you must take great care, Miss D'Arblay, not to contract a chill in these ballrooms, which can be terribly drafty as well as stiflingly hot," the lady at her side commented, bestowing upon her a smile. "It is the worst possible combination of situations, I find."

"I am quite comfortable, I assure you," Serafina replied, feeling uncomfortable, for she had no notion her shudder had been such a profound one.

"Only last Season Lady Darnborough contracted a chill at a ball at Holland House, from which she didn't recover. She expired three days later. . . ."

Her elderly companion's reminiscences were fortunately interrupted by an altercation at the other side of the ballroom. It caused Serafina to be diverted from discomforting thoughts about Imogen, or indeed ladies who contract fatal chills at balls.

A slightly built woman with fair curls fashionably cropped and a man who sported a careless elegance were in the midst of a violent quarrel, not caring who overheard or indeed overlooked the altercation, as many were doing with great amusement. After a moment the young woman hitched up her skirts and flounced out of the ballroom, and the gentleman in some apparent bewilderment ran one hand through his unruly curls. Then he turned on his heel and followed her out of the room, leaving the countless onlookers to discuss the incident excitedly among themselves.

The lady sitting next to Serafina chuckled, observing, "It is altercations of this kind that liven up these dull evenings."

"Dull?" Serafina responded in surprise. "How odd you should think so. I don't find it in the least dull."

"It is quite apparent to me you have not attended many."

"Well, no . . ." Serafina was bound to admit.

"You will soon grow weary of them, I fear. All these diversions are so similar. The same people. Even the food does not vary overmuch. However, for most of us, seeing Lord Byron and Caro Lamb having one of their kickups makes the evening worthwhile."

Serafina gasped and then laughed out loud. "Was that Lord Byron, the great poet?"

The woman looked amused. "You must be the only person in London who does not know Caro Lamb is in the midst of a volatile relationship with our wonder poet."

"Oh, what a pity. I had hoped to engage him in conversation at some point. I do admire his work."

"No doubt it was just such a conversation that has sparked Lady Lamb into one of her pelters. She is inordinately jealous of any female his lordship addresses, even if they speak to him first."

Serafina looked disappointed. "I had looked to see far loftier behavior from a gentleman of his literary prowess."

The lady laughed. "How odd you should think so, my dear. The more outrageously a gentleman behaves, the better he is considered by his peers." As she glanced across the room, she began to put away her sewing. "Come along, dear. Supper is being served. It won't do to dawdle, for when everyone goes on the scramble very little is left."

There was a great deal of food left when Serafina began to fill her plate. All manner of delicious morsels were on offer. Chicken pieces, lobster mousse, turbot, and salads. However, as she made her choice, her usually robust appetite for once deserted her.

She allowed her plate to be filled with tasty tidbits, but found she had little desire to consume them. When she glanced around, she caught sight of Imogen in conversation with one of the young men with whom she had danced earlier, which afforded her some measure of relief. They seemed to be enjoying a relaxed conversation. If Imogen was not meant for Jolyon, then better she should be settled with one of these young bucks than someone like Lord Trenton, who she felt would not be in the least suitable for her friend.

As she glanced around for somewhere to put her

supper plate, an unfamiliar voice said, "Allow me to take that for you, ma'am."

When she turned on her heel, she found herself looking at Lord Trenton's perfectly folded neck cloth. How Jolyon would admire his style, was her first involuntary thought.

With perfect aplomb he deposited the plate on a nearby table and, taking her arm, he led her somewhat unwillingly into a corner, saying in a soft voice, "Our previous acquaintance means I need no formal introduction to you, although it is time for us to meet in a more proper manner than our other encounter allowed. I believe I have the honor of addressing Miss Serafina D'Arblay."

"Indeed," she murmured, swallowing noisily and sketching a curtsy that at least allowed her to conceal, momentarily, her discomposure.

"Robert Trenton. Your servant, ma'am."

"I caught sight of you dancing with Miss Geddes a short while ago."

"That was a great pleasure. Miss Geddes speaks highly of you."

"I am obliged to her," she answered, avoiding looking directly at him.

One or two people nearby were taking note of the conversation and appeared surprised that he was to be seen addressing so dowdy a female. At least that was how they appeared to look to Serafina.

"My behavior the other day was not normal for me." He paused, and her eyes remained downcast. "It was, I own, a trifle outrageous, and in mitigation my only excuse is that I was disconcerted by being given a setdown by so young a girl."

"I am no young girl, my lord. I am five and twenty, but I do confess that I, too, should not have spoken so freely. Therefore, you have no need whatsoever to beg my pardon."

"I would not normally do so, but as Miss Geddes speaks of you with such fondness, I considered it incumbent of me to make an exception."

When she looked at him, she realized at last the reason for his apology. He was afraid she would speak ill of him to Imogen, and perhaps had already told her of the ill-mannered buck she had encountered on the day of their arrival.

"You really have no need to do so, my lord. I had quite forgotten the incident until you reminded me of it. It was, after all, the most trifling matter."

He smiled, a smile that she acknowledged could be winning. If he was truly in search of a wife, he would have no trouble gaining the devotion of a naive girl just come out.

"I am utterly relieved to hear you say so," he replied, and she detected a hint of insincerity in his manner that angered her anew.

"I feel I must warn you, my lord," she said quickly, before her courage failed her, "if you are intent upon paying court to Miss Geddes, she has already lost her heart to another."

After she had spoken, she drew in a sharp breath, afraid that she had been too hasty, but he appeared as urbane as ever. "The gentleman is to be envied," he told her, revealing neither shock nor surprise.

Serafina supposed he was so sure of his own charms, he could not regard any other gentleman as a rival.

"I hear the music striking up," he said a moment later as the supper room began to empty. "Will you do me the honor of standing up with me for the country dance, Miss D'Arblay?"

Serafina almost shrank back in alarm, glancing around, fearing that the guests would be staring at her in horror, but they were, for the most part, indulging in their own conversations or making their way back into the ballroom.

"No!" she gasped. "I mean, I cannot. I should not."

He looked amused, and she supposed he would regard her as a country bumpkin, good for a laugh with his cronies later on.

"Why should you not stand up with me? This is your cousin's house, I believe. Where better place to sport a toe? Unless, of course, you are already engaged for this set." She made a strangled noise in her throat, for he must surely know there was no such possibility. "Then, I can only assume," he continued, "you have not forgiven me for what passed between us the other day."

At this point Serafina was beginning to feel rather hot. "It is not for me to forgive, my lord, even if there was something that needed my forgiveness, which I assure you there is not."

"The accident really was not my fault," he told her as he led her out of the supper room, giving her no further opportunity to refuse.

When they passed Caroline, she smiled impishly at them. Wallace's demeanor did not alter, but Serafina fancied he looked slightly surprised to see his dowdy cousin on the arm of such a pink of the *ton*.

The dance began the moment they joined the set,

and as Serafina had already observed, he was a fine dancer. She suspected he was the kind of man who excelled at all he did, a thought that did not endear him to her.

When the dance was over, he escorted her to the side of the room and bowed. "Until our next encounter, ma'am. May it be as pleasant as this one."

As he moved away to be swallowed up by the crowds, Serafina took a deep breath, feeling she had undergone an ordeal, which was nonsense, for several ladies nearby were eyeing her with both envy and curiosity. She smiled at them shyly but had little time to recover her demeanor before Lady Wolcot came striding up to her, her face a mask of fury.

"Just what do you consider you are about, Miss D'Arblay?" she demanded.

Serafina regarded her with new alarm. "My lady?"

"Don't act the little innocent with me, my girl, for I won't have it. You were just seen to be dancing with Lord Trenton."

"Yes . . ." Serafina replied, continuing to look bewildered.

"Am I obliged to remind you that you are not here to flaunt yourself in front of gentlemen? It is most unbecoming of you."

"Flaunt?" Serafina protested. "But, my lady, I assure you I did no such . . ."

"Yes, flaunt! Why else would Lord Trenton feel obliged to ask you—a paid companion—to stand up with him for a country dance? Or did you flaunt your relationship to our host instead?"

"Lady Wolcot, I believe Lord Trenton asked me only to ingratiate himself with Imogen."

The countess's lip curled. "What humgumption. Since when has any gentleman, let alone one of the caliber of Lord Trenton, used a paid companion to ingratiate himself with the woman of his choice? Really, Miss D'Arblay, that is a Canterbury Tale if ever I heard one."

Serafina took a deep breath before saying, "I assure you, I did not intend to offend anyone."

"I am bound to confess I am grievously disappointed in you. I do trust you will not continue in this unseemly behavior, for if you do, I feel it only fair to counsel you that you will be very sorry. Lord Trenton will only look upon you as a bit of muslin if you continue to encourage him in such a shameless manner."

Serafina gasped, hardly able to believe that one innocent dance in which she had participated so unwillingly, could bring forth this flow of invective. It was suddenly clear to her that so anxious was Lady Wolcot to have the viscount as Imogen's husband, she saw rivals where they could not possibly exist. There seemed no point in attempting to reason with her.

"I really do beg your pardon, my lady," Serafina said, her eyes downcast in as reasonable a facsimile of a penitent as she could contrive. "Be assured it will not occur again."

Some of the countess's wrath faded then. "I am relieved to hear you say so. It would give me no pleasure to harbor a strumpet beneath my roof."

At this statement Serafina lost most of her deference and would have said something rash, only Imogen came up to them, her eyes bright, her cheeks flushed with excitement.

"Is this not the most wonderful evening? I have not been obliged to sit out even one set. And you, Serafina, you slyboots, I saw you standing up with Lord Trenton."

"I have just informed Miss D'Arblay that it was most unseemly of her," Lady Wolcot said, and some of Imogen's pleasure immediately faded.

"Oh, dear. I fear I am the one at fault, my lady, not Serafina."

The countess's brow furrowed. "How is that so?"

"I mentioned to his lordship that it was a pity my friend, Miss D'Arblay, who was such an excellent dancer, should be obliged to sit out all the sets, and he was all condescension and agreement. . . ."

Serafina felt a flush of humiliation permeate her cheeks, and then Imogen chattered on. "How glad I am he is not fat or gouty. Not that I look upon him as a true suitor, but he is much more charming than I envisaged. I have even made the acquaintance of his sister, Lady Betteridge, who is quite toplofty but condescending, I own."

"I do trust you did not prattle on to her in that cork-brained manner," Lady Wolcot said severely, which caused some of Imogen's brightness to dull.

"How glad I am to see you enjoying yourself so greatly, dearest," Serafina said quickly.

"How I wish Jolyon was here to enjoy it, too."

"Jolyon?" Lady Wolcot asked sharply. "*Who* pray is Jolyon?"

"My brother, my lady," Serafina explained. "He and Imogen were great friends in Coverdale."

"A chawbacon would scarce fit in at this kind of

diversion, no more than you do, Miss D'Arblay." So saying she swept away.

Imogen gasped. "How can she call Jolyon a chawbacon?"

"She does not know him," Serafina said sadly, "and I fear my behavior this evening has put her in a miff."

"*I* am delighted you danced with Lord Trenton, and where better place than in your cousin's house?"

"Lord Trenton said something in a similar vein, but in the future, Imogen, I do beg you not to solicit partners on my behalf. It will not do."

The girl looked not in the least repentant. "We must have a coze later and discuss all that has happened tonight. Now, I must go and dance a minuet with Sir Philip Chorton. How I wish it was the waltz!"

"You must not on any account accept an invitation to a waltz," Serafina told her quickly as she hurried away.

"Yes, I know. Is it not a pity?"

Serafina smiled at her encouragingly, but once she had gone, the smile faded, too, and she wondered if her position at Wolcot House would become totally untenable before long if Lady Wolcot insisted upon mistaking her every deed.

# SIX

The fact that Imogen seemed to have dismissed Lord Trenton as a suitor comforted Serafina somewhat, although she was fully aware that in the time to come his charm could quite easily win her over. Imogen did not have sufficient strength of will or sophistication to withstand all he had to offer her, especially if Lady Wolcot continually supported his suit as she was bound to do.

In retrospect, Serafina was also able to understand the countess's anger toward her. It must have looked very much as if she was casting out lures to be invited to stand up with one of the most eligible gentlemen in the room while others, more well connected and socially prominent, were obliged to sit at the side of the dance floor.

No one could have been aware that she had been pressed to stand up with him against her will. No one would have believed her had she protested that this was so. She was certain almost all of the ladies present would have gladly changed places with her, not knowing she had hated every moment of the time she had spent with him. It was a great relief to her that she was unlikely to find herself in his company in the future. Lady Wolcot would make certain of that, and Serafina could only be glad of it.

However, accompanying Imogen on her frequent shopping excursions was something she found she did enjoy. The shops in London were a novelty to them both, and although she was able to buy little, she certainly liked helping Imogen choose the items necessary for a successful Season, and such expeditions diverted her mind from all that troubled her of late.

On this particular occasion, however, Serafina had been persuaded to spend some of her precious salary on a much-needed paisley shawl.

"The one you possess is shabby and almost threadbare," Imogen pointed out. "It might have done in the country, but you really cannot go about London in such a dowdy manner."

The shawl they had been admiring was very beautiful, in colors that would complement most of her gowns, and with Imogen's urging she had at last been unable to resist the temptation of a rare purchase for herself.

They enjoyed the expedition so much, the two young ladies went on to view the marvels on display at Sir John Soane's Museum. On most days Imogen was as eager as Serafina to see as many of the sights of London as their time allowed. So far they had contrived to visit the menagerie at the Tower of London, but had proclaimed it dull, Lord Elgin's exhibition of ancient Greek marbles at his home in Park Lane, and paid their shillings to see the wonderful paintings on display at Somerset House by painters of the Royal Academy.

"How amazing some of the exhibits are," Imogen enthused as they returned from the museum.

"I did enjoy all the Egyptian artifacts," Serafina admitted.

"How odd the Egyptians must have been to mummify their dead! It's so gruesome!"

"No doubt they would have considered us odd for our burial rites. Your papa will be delighted to learn you are improving your mind, Imogen."

The girl chuckled. "If only I didn't miss everyone at home, life in London would be quite sublime."

"I'm persuaded all those you left at home at Coverdale will be missing you equally as much, Imogen."

The girl dimpled at the thought and then played with her gloves for a moment or two before venturing, "Did you contrive to form an opinion of Sir Philip Chorton the other evening?"

"Alas I did not have the opportunity, but from his appearance he seemed . . . presentable."

Imogen smiled to herself. "I found him diverting, I am bound to confess. He has offered to take me riding in Hyde Park just as soon as his new high-perch phaeton is delivered."

Serafina's spirits suddenly plummeted. She held fast to the hope, vain as it might be, that Imogen would, through all the diversions, flattery, and temptations, remain true to Jolyon.

Then Imogen cast her a sidelong glance. "Although you had no opportunity to speak to Sir

Philip, you did, however, have ample opportunity to judge Lord Trenton."

Serafina laughed mirthlessly. "Shall I ever forget that dreadful evening after Lady Wolcot's vapors?"

"That was all nonsense, as I'm sure she will now own. No doubt you did contrive to form an opinion about him during your coze."

"It was no coze, Imogen, I assure you. We danced just the one time, and we spoke mainly of what politeness decrees in such circumstances. Had you not prevailed upon him to stand up with me, I doubt if he would be aware of my existence."

Serafina could not prevent a note of bitterness creeping into her voice. It appeared that her friend was unaware of it, for she said, a trifle coyly, "Come now, dearest, you must have been able to form some kind of opinion of him. Oh, Serafina, you know how I value your opinion. Indeed, I rely upon it. Everything here seems to happen so fast, and in an overwhelming manner. I cannot help but be bewildered. I am flattered by his attention to me, naturally, but I cannot conceive that someone as sophisticated as Lord Trenton would be interested in the likes of me."

Serafina put one of her gloved hands on her friend's. "My dear, you have no notion how fetching you are—everyone agrees upon that—and you have the correct breeding, let alone your portion, so if Lord Trenton is hanging out for a wife, why should it not be you? He certainly is a catch and appeared to be more than a little interested in you the other evening. That is my opinion of the matter for what it is worth."

Imogen looked rather more dismayed than pleased. Serafina was not entirely surprised. Anyone who became Lady Trenton would be obliged to hold a prestigious position in society, but she had no reason to suppose the viscount would not be an indulgent husband. She just suspected that someone as cynical as Lord Trenton might in time grow weary of the very qualities that had attracted him to her.

By the time they arrived back at Wolcot House, the two young women were chattering lightheartedly once again, the problems of courtship and matrimony put out of their minds for the present. More pressing was the selection of a gown to wear to the Betteridges' rout. For Serafina, at least, the decision was an easy one, for she had very little choice.

When they entered the hall of Wolcot House, Popplewell, for once, did not bestow upon them his usual smile. "Her ladyship has asked for you to join her in the red drawing room as soon as you return, ladies."

"Does she require me to join her?" Serafina asked in some surprise, for she had become adept in avoiding Lady Wolcot as much as was possible since the night of the Wyndhams' soiree.

"Yes, ma'am," the house steward replied.

"Botheration!" Imogen exclaimed. "I had hoped to spend an hour before dinner reading the book I borrowed from the circulating library this morning. I have no doubt at all," she went on as they hurried up the stairs, "she merely wishes to regale me with all the wonderful places to which we have been invited."

"If that is so, it is not likely she would ask me to join you. Almost all the invitations you have received do not include my name."

"In my opinion that is a great pity."

"I am more than content to remain here," Serafina told her truthfully.

The moment the footman ushered them into the room, Lady Wolcot got to her feet, and it was evident from her demeanor she was in something of a pelter. "I have been awaiting your arrival for some time," she announced.

"I do beg your pardon, my lady," Imogen replied. "We have been out for an unconscionable time, but we were enjoying ourselves exceedingly."

"As you can see, I am in a great fidge to have words with you."

"We have been improving our minds," Imogen went on.

"Let no one say you are not in need of some improvement in that direction," her godmother replied before going on quickly. "There is no manner in which I can say this any other way, but several of my snuffboxes are missing."

Both young ladies gasped. Sure enough, there were several gaps among the collection, and from one glance Serafina could see clearly it was those of the greatest value that were missing.

"How dreadful," Imogen responded. "You must be quite overset."

"It is indeed tragic," Serafina agreed. "Has a thorough search been made?"

Lady Wolcot's lip curled, and her bosom swelled. "The house has been searched from top to bottom. Nothing has been overlooked, I assure you, but there is no sign of them anywhere."

Imogen looked somewhat bewildered. "What does it mean?"

"I think her ladyship is trying to say they have been stolen," Serafina told her gently.

As Imogen gasped, the countess looked triumphant. "That, I regret to say, is the only solution that comes to mind."

"Oh . . ." Imogen gasped again. "How dreadful to contemplate. To think of someone sneaking in here, perhaps while we slept . . ."

As she began to shake, Serafina put one arm around her shoulders. "Now, now, dearest. There is no cause for you to get into a pucker over this."

"Do you have any suggestions as to the solution of this mystery, Miss D'Arblay?" the countess asked.

Serafina had been staring at the table and the awful spaces left by the missing snuffboxes, and when Lady Wolcot spoke to her, she turned around quickly. "I wish I could help."

"You could assist by returning them to me now, and nothing more will be said on the matter."

Imogen recoiled, her eyes wide. "Oh no . . ." she gasped. "You cannot possibly mean . . ."

Serafina looked bewildered. "My lady, I have no notion where they are. Why should I?"

"You are the newcomer here."

"Surely that is no cause to believe I . . ."

"Nothing has ever gone missing before, and you

are known to be in need of funds. You are also sensible enough to be aware you are never likely to earn sufficient to provide for your brother as you so desperately wish to do."

All the while she was speaking, Serafina fought hard to contain both her anger and her fear. "However needy I happened to be, I would not steal, I assure you."

"My dear," the countess answered, drawing a deep sigh, "you must see the matter from my point of view. I certainly don't wish to accuse you, but there is no one else."

"It could have been one of the servants," Imogen suggested.

"No," Serafina contradicted quickly, feeling sure all her friends below stairs were entirely trustworthy.

Lady Wolcot evidently agreed, for she replied, "They have all been with me a very long time. If you were anyone else but Mr. Wyndham's cousin, I should feel obliged to call in the constable to investigate the matter to its conclusion. If you are adamant in declaring your innocence . . ."

"I am!"

"Then I am obliged to be satisfied with that, but you cannot possibly expect to remain beneath my roof. You should return to Coverdale and the protection of your aunt. I am persuaded you want a scandal no more than I do."

By this time Serafina was wringing her hands in anguish. "Lady Wolcot, I beg you to listen to me. I did not steal your snuffboxes. You have my word upon that."

"I have no notion what worth your word involves."

"Even though I cannot pretend to suspect who did steal your property, I feel it unfair that I should be singled out for suspicion. It is as if you had quite made up your mind before I arrived back."

"As I am sure you appreciate, Miss D'Arblay, there is no one else to suspect. I am assured there is no sign of forced entry."

"Oh Serafina," Imogen wailed, tears filling her blue eyes, "you did buy the shawl this morning."

"With my own money!" she retorted. "Imogen, you cannot possibly believe this tarradiddle."

The girl shook her head tearfully. "Of course not, dearest. I am a complete chucklehead. There must be some other explanation of their disappearance. I *know* there is!"

"Imogen go to your room before you become too distraught," Lady Wolcot ordered.

"I cannot leave while this matter is unresolved."

"Be certain it is resolved. Now, do as you are bid. I am sufficiently out of patience without being faced with a disobedient goddaughter. Go along, *now*!"

Imogen cast Serafina a regretful look and then slowly moved across the room. When she reached the door, she paused to look back again.

"Mayhap it would be best for you to go home to Coverdale, Serafina. When her ladyship recovers the snuffboxes, you will be able to return."

"The chit is correct, Miss D'Arblay," the countess explained when Imogen closed the door behind her.

"And if you do not recover the snuffboxes, ma'am?" Serafina asked in a bitter tone.

"That will be unfortunate for both of us."

"I shall always remain branded a thief! Do you realize the severity of that to one of my calling?" When the countess made no reply, Serafina went on, unable to hide her distress, "I believe you are a very vindictive woman, Lady Wolcot."

"If I were, Miss D'Arblay, you would now be on your way to Newgate. I believe I have been more than merciful to such an ingrate. Now, be pleased to go immediately from my house. Your bags are packed and awaiting you downstairs."

Serafina gasped. "You presumed my guilt with not a shred of proof or even waiting to hear me plead my innocence. That is not my notion of justice, ma'am."

Lady Wolcot turned her back on Serafina, and it was clear there was nothing more to be done or said. No amount of reasoning would prevail.

As she fled the room, Serafina was close to tears. She ran down the stairs and was almost blinded by the tears she refused to shed.

"Shall I call a hackney carriage for you, ma'am?" Popplewell asked in a gentle voice.

She nodded, unable to trust herself to speak at that moment, and a footman hurried to hail the hackney as Popplewell helped her on with her pelisse. She tied her bonnet ribbons with a less than steady hand, unable to look at any of the servants, who must know she was suspected of the awful crime.

"If it is of any consolation to you, ma'am, none

of us believe you to be guilty," the house steward told her, looking a trifle embarrassed.

She nodded her thanks, aware of the invidious position in which the servants found themselves. She didn't doubt Popplewell's sincerity, but she was certain he was also relieved that none of them were under suspicion.

Her two meager boxes were loaded into the hackney carriage when it arrived. Just as Serafina was about to climb in, she glanced back to the house to see Imogen hovering in the hall, her face pale and full of despair. Up until that moment Serafina had been concerned with what this accusation would mean to her, but belatedly she realized it also meant that she had failed Imogen, leaving her to Lady Wolcot's sole ministrations in this her come-out year.

There was absolutely nothing she could do about the matter, and Serafina just raised her hand in a gesture of farewell.

When the jarvey asked, "Where to, miss?" she answered with a profound sigh, "Take me to Wyndham House in Piccadilly."

# SEVEN

"I regret that Mrs. Wyndham is not at home at present," the house steward informed her the moment she stepped into the hall of Wyndham House.

The lackey as he spoke glanced contemptuously at the hem of her gown to which a straw from the floor of the hackney carriage still adhered. Few visitors to Wyndham House would arrive by that mode of transport.

"However, shall I inquire if Mr. Wyndham will receive you, ma'am?"

"If you please," Serafina replied, striving hard to curtail her agitation. "Tell him his cousin, Miss D'Arblay, wishes to see him on a matter of great import."

A few minutes later she was being ushered into Wallace's library. He was seated behind his desk before a pile of documents that looked somewhat official and involved. Not for Wallace Wyndham the giddy world of continuous pleasure. He paid assiduous attention to financial affairs, and as a consequence grew richer by the year.

"Serafina!" he exclaimed as he rose to his feet.

"What is so important it brings you here at this time of the day?"

"Wallace, I do beg your pardon for troubling you. I can see you are well-occupied by matters of business, and you may be sure I would not impose upon you unless the matter was one of great import, but something dreadful has happened. I'm really in the suds and in need of your assistance."

A shadow crossed his face. "What can be so bad it's put you under the hatches?"

"I have been turned out of Wolcot House!"

Again she wrung her hands together, but her cousin merely looked wry. "Has that sharp tongue of yours got the better of you again?"

"No! Oh, Wallace, don't roast me now, I beg of you. Lady Wolcot has accused me . . . of stealing some of her snuffboxes."

The shock of revelation registered immediately on his face. "My stars! This really is a case of pickles."

"Needless to say," she added, her head held high, "I am innocent."

He laughed then. "You are nothing if not totally honest, Serafina, as I know to my cost. Lady Wolcot always did have more hair than wit, and I don't doubt her snuffboxes are nothing more than vulgar gewgaws. Well, what's to do my dear? I take it you can't prove you didn't do the dastardly deed?"

"Nor can she prove that I did, and I beg you don't treat this matter lightly."

"Wouldn't dream of it, my dear," he answered in a tone she didn't entirely trust. He stroked his chin thoughtfully for a moment or two before asking, "What would you have me do about it?"

"Wallace, may I stay here with you and Caroline?"

Once again he exhibited considerable surprise. "Why the deuce do you want to do that? You only came to London because of Imogen, and if you are not acting as her companion, you'd be best served going back to Mama at Wyndham House."

"You are obtuse, Wallace. Can't you see that if I go back to the country now, it will look as if I am guilty!"

"As far as I can observe, there is nothing you can do to prove your innocence if you do stay here with us. Well, reluctant as I am to say so, my dear, having you as a resident here will not reflect well upon us. You really must see how it would affect us."

"Wallace, you are a humbug," she retorted, stamping her foot upon the floor in her frustration.

"Oh, come now, Serafina, there is no use in flying out at me. While you are on your high ropes, you cannot reason at all. Not that I entirely blame you, of course. This has been a most dreadful shock to you."

She laughed without mirth. "That, my dear coz, is something of an understatement."

"Allow me to know what is best for you," he said soothingly. "Go back to Mama, and I'll wager Rosemary Lane to a rag shop those deuced gewgaws will be found somewhere, and that bird-witted female will be throwing herself at your feet, begging your forgiveness before you've had time to unpack your boxes."

"You will have to forgive me if I do not wager upon that eventuality," Serafina replied, moving toward the door. "I must have had windmills in my head to think you might come to my assistance. I might as well bark at the moon."

The young man started after her. "Don't let us part brass rags, Serafina. Nothing can be gained by your staying in London, I assure you. Here, allow me to pay for your coach journey."

"No, thank you, Wallace," she told him, pausing by the door. "I don't need your ten pieces of silver. I can afford to pay for my own coach journey—just."

He smiled in a conciliatory manner. "Now, that is what I call sensible. Everything will soon be as right as a trivet. You'll see."

By the time she went out into the street, Serafina was no longer angry; she was despairing, knowing there was no manner in which she could clear her name, and the injustice of the situation was well nigh unbearable.

Just outside Wyndham House stood one of the new gaslights that were now appearing in the capital, and while she waited for a hackney carriage to pass by, she leaned against it, tears streaming down her face unchecked at last.

Many carriages, built for speed and driven by young bucks, came too close to her, but she remained uncaring of the danger they posed. It was, at least, dry on the road, which meant she was not constantly splashed, although it was likely she would have remained unaware of that, too.

When a curricle drove by her and then began to slow, she did not notice it, so deep was her despair.

A few moments later an all too familiar voice was calling her name.

"Miss D'Arblay! It is Miss D'Arblay, isn't it?"

As Lord Trenton walked back down the road toward her, Serafina hastily wiped away her tears with her gloved fingers and averted her face, for she could not disguise her distress.

"Miss D'Arblay, how unexpected to find you . . ."

His smile faded, and she knew she must look absolutely terrible. Her hair had become unkempt after taking her bonnet off and then putting it on again with no heed to the state of her curls. Her face would undoubtedly be streaked by her tears, but she affected a watery smile in the hope he would not notice her distress.

"My lord."

"Miss D'Arblay, forgive me for saying so, but you . . . look discomposed. Can I be of any assistance to you?" When she merely shook her head, he asked, "Is anything amiss?"

"I have been waiting an unconscionable time for a hackney carriage," she told him, by way of explanation.

He looked somewhat relieved. "If that is what troubles you, you must wait no longer. I shall drive you back to Wolcot House with no further delay."

"Oh no!" she gasped, recoiling slightly. "I mean . . . I am not going to Wolcot House."

"It makes no matter, for I shall take you wherever you wish to go."

"I am going to the Swan to catch the evening coach to Winchester."

He frowned then. "Are you returning home?" She

nodded and bit her lip. "This is very sudden, is it not?"

"Yes," she answered.

"Forgive me once again for asking, Miss D'Arblay, but you do appear to be in some considerable distress. Are you, by any chance, indisposed?"

"Not at all, you may be certain. Do not, I beg of you, concern yourself on my behalf."

Once more she affected a smile, but unbidden the tears filled her eyes instead and began to roll down her cheeks. No effort could hold them back now. She had been treated so unjustly, she could hardly bear it.

"I fear that something has incommoded you, ma'am," he persisted, frowning again.

A moment later he handed her his lawn handkerchief. When she hesitated to take it, he did not withdraw it, and she accepted it at last.

Within a sennight all London would know, she reasoned. Lady Wolcot would delight in denouncing her as a thief to her cronies. It would make a delightful *on-dit.*

"I have been turned out by Lady Wolcot," she told him at last, dabbing at her eyes with the handkerchief.

"What reason did she give?" he asked tersely.

"She accused me of stealing her snuffboxes."

"Surely you are bamming me."

She looked directly at him at last. "Do I look as if I am, my lord?"

"No, Miss D'Arblay." The silence that followed lasted a few seconds, and then he said in a more brisk manner, "I believe I would like to hear more of this matter, and this is not the most congenial place for us to converse. Come with me."

"I cannot, for I don't wish to miss the stage. I have nowhere to stay tonight . . ."

"The coaching inn is not far from here. I shall convey you there myself after you are a little recovered. Where are your belongings?"

"At my cousin's house."

He appeared about to comment, but then he led her to the curricle, helped her onto the box, and then tooled into Wallace Wyndham's carriage drive where he instructed his tiger to load on the boxes.

A very few minutes later he drove into a similar drive in front of a house that appeared even larger than her cousin's. For some time Serafina had felt numb with misery, but now she raised her head and frowned at her strange surroundings.

"Where have you brought me?"

"This is my sister's house. Lady Betteridge. I don't believe it wise, even in these circumstances, for you to come unchaperoned to my house. The tattle-baskets are only too ready to make mischief on the slightest pretext."

"Will your sister not mind if you bring a stranger into her house?"

"I think not. You will find her sympathetic."

When they entered the hall, he indicated she should be seated on a settle in an alcove while he handed his beaver hat, coat, and gloves to the startled house steward.

"If you'll be seated, ma'am, I shall endeavor to locate my sister."

"Her ladyship is not yet returned, my lord," the

lackey informed him, "and Sir Arthur is ensconced with his books. Mayhap you would have me announce you."

The viscount laughed. "Oh no, Dillon, I know better than to disturb Sir Arthur just now."

Serafina had only just seated herself in the alcove when an extremely beautiful and elegant lady swept in. As she did so, she pulled off her stylish bonnet, and when her eyes alighted on Lord Trenton, her face broke into a smile of genuine pleasure.

"Robert, dearest! What a pleasant surprise this is. I did not look to see you today." She kissed him lightly on the cheek. "I have had the most harrowing afternoon imaginable, listening to Betsy Melbourne lament her daughter-in-law's behavior. Caro is still totally infatuated with Byron, who is naturally flattered by her tiresome attentions. But, do you know, Robert? I believe Caro Lamb is a little—well—unbalanced. Poor William is quite beside himself, and Lady Melbourne is at a total loss as to what to do about the wretched affair. It is such a public affair. Betsy blames Caro entirely, and I am inclined to agree."

Suddenly she caught sight of Serafina, sitting pale-faced in the alcove, the handkerchief clutched in her hands, which were clasped tightly in her lap, her eyes downcast.

"Good grief! Robert, who . . . ?"

"Mira, this is Miss D'Arblay, an acquaintance of mine." A knowing look came into Lady Betteridge's eyes, and her brother went on quickly, "No, Mira, it is not what you think. I have just found

Miss D'Arblay in some distress nearby and hoped you would offer her some tea."

With no further ado Lady Betteridge gave the order for tea to be served in the drawing room, but she continued to look rather perplexed, something for which Serafina could not blame her.

She felt she had been imposing before, but now she certainly did not want to be regarded as one of Lord Trenton's lightskirts. It was enough to be considered a thief. She stood up abruptly, saying, "You are both being very kind, but I feel I must not impose upon your time any longer."

"My dear, if my brother requests me to give you tea, I do not doubt he has a very good reason for doing so."

Then Serafina found herself being hurried up the stairs and into a small drawing room decorated in which she now recognized to be an Egyptian theme. The decor was a great deal more restrained than what she had become accustomed to at Lady Wolcot's house.

A few moments after they had entered the drawing room, footmen arrived with the silver kettle, fine china, and the caddy whereupon Lady Betteridge proceeded to make the tea. It was Lord Trenton who handed Serafina her cup, and she was perturbed to discover it rattled in the saucer as she took it from him.

The viscount went to stand in front of the fire screen. On the wall above him the portrait of a stern-looking gentleman looked down on them.

"Do you feel you are able to elaborate upon what

you told me outside, Miss D'Arblay?" he asked in a gentle voice that almost started her tears again.

"Mayhap Miss D'Arblay would prefer me to leave," Lady Betteridge suggested.

"No, ma'am," Serafina assured her. "It makes no odds who knows about this wretched affair now, for I do not doubt Lady Wolcot will tell everyone as soon as possible."

"I own to be intrigued," she replied, lifting the cup to her lips.

As quickly as she could, Serafina related the awful events that followed her return to Wolcot House that afternoon.

Lady Betteridge gasped and put her cup down on the table. "How shocking for you, my dear."

Her brother listened carefully, and his expression remained inscrutable throughout. When Serafina finished the sorry tale, he asked, "Why did Lady Wolcot accuse you, Miss D'Arblay?"

"There was no one else, and I am poor, I suppose. In her eyes that was motive enough."

"That dreadful woman," Lady Betteridge murmured. "I always considered her unspeakably vulgar."

"Has she any evidence against you?" Lord Trenton asked.

"No, I don't believe she has, other than my being the only person she wished to suspect." Serafina turned to Lady Betteridge to explain. "For some reason I cannot comprehend, Lady Wolcot took me in dislike at the outset of my stay."

"She has many servants in her house who may even be poorer than you and with as much opportunity to steal her property," Lady Betteridge suggested.

"No," Serafina told her firmly. "I do not believe for one moment it was one of them."

Lady Betteridge looked surprised. "It is astonishing that you should say so, ma'am, in the circumstances."

"I have come to know them all, and I believe they are as much beyond reproach as I am."

"That opinion does you much credit," her ladyship responded, glancing at her brother.

"When I came upon you outside," he said in a studied manner, "had you approached your cousin for help?" Serafina nodded. "To no avail, I presume?" Once again she nodded.

"Is Wallace Wyndham your cousin?" Lady Betteridge asked, looking astonished.

"Yes. He did not believe in my guilt, but he thought I should return to my aunt's house in the country."

"You evidently wished to remain in London," the viscount suggested, putting down his own empty teacup.

Serafina cast him a beseeching look. "How else can I hope to prove my innocence? Not that there is much chance of that even if I could stay."

Lady Betteridge clucked her tongue. "What a sorry tale this is to be sure, and Mr. Wyndham is nothing if not a quiz to treat you in so cavalier a fashion after all you have been obliged to endure today."

Serafina sipped at the cooling tea at last. "I can appreciate his point of view, my lady. It would be devilishly awkward to have me, an alleged felon, beneath his roof."

"But the accusation is based upon nothing more than Lady Wolcot's prejudice," Lady Betteridge protested. "It is so unfair."

Serafina smiled faintly, warming to her. "Thank you, my lady, but Lady Wolcot does not perceive it as unfair. She truly believes I have stolen her property, and anyone she tells will assume I am . . . a thief." Suddenly she paled. "Oh, how am I going to tell Jolyon?"

The viscount frowned. "Jolyon?"

"My brother. He relies upon me so. I cannot bear to tell him. He will be devastated."

"This is going to injure your attempt to find another position, is it not?" Lord Trenton asked.

Again she nodded. "I shall just be obliged to throw myself on my aunt's charity, although that will not be easy for me."

"You have been acting as companion to Miss Geddes, have you not?" Lady Betteridge inquired.

"That is only until she is married. I am an experienced archivist. I catalog old papers and libraries."

Lady Betteridge looked both surprised and impressed, and then she looked at her brother. "Well, Robert, now we have heard what Miss D'Arblay has to tell us, what are we to do?"

For a moment he did not answer, and then he said, "I suppose I had best have words with Wallace Wyndham. He must be made to face his obligations to you, ma'am."

Serafina looked alarmed. "Oh no! No! You must

not on any account approach my cousin! In any event I would not wish to live under his roof upon sufferance, for that is all it would be." She got to her feet, looking from one to the other. "You have both been so kind, and I do appreciate that, but I believe it best if I go now. If you'd be kind enough to call me a hackney carriage . . ."

Lady Betteridge also got to her feet. "No, my dear. When I first saw you, you were in a terrible bobble. I insist you have more tea. Bring me your cup, and I shall refill it."

Obediently Serafina did so, for she needed little persuasion. The prospect of a coach journey and all its rigors was not inviting. Less inviting was the necessity of throwing herself on her aunt's mercy. Not that her aunt would turn her out. Her Aunt Wyndham had always done her duty by her sister's orphaned children, but Serafina's pride made acceptance difficult.

As she sat down again with her second cup of tea, Lady Betteridge said, glancing at each of them in turn, "Pray excuse me for a short while. I shall return presently."

After she had gone, there was a long silence in the room. Serafina stared down at her cup, aware that Lord Trenton was studying her intently, and his brow was slightly furrowed.

"You really had no need to go to this trouble on my behalf," she said when the silence became onerous. "I fear that I have incommoded Lady Betteridge."

"She is too good-natured to turn away anyone in need of help," he replied, "and occasionally—not very often mind—I feel a strange urge to put forward the better side of my nature."

Serafina looked up sharply then and saw he was smiling. "You're roasting me," she accused, feeling foolish.

"At least I have contrived to make you smile again."

"I feel I should point out to you that if Lady Wolcot discovers you have come to my aid, she will be most displeased."

At this statement he threw back his head and laughed. "My dear Miss D'Arblay, do you really think I care a fig what that piece of overlaced mutton thinks or says of me?"

"No, I do not, but she is, in effect, Imogen's guardian while she is in London, and I would not like to think it would go ill between you and her because of me."

A hard look came into his eyes. "If you believe Lady Wolcot's ambitions for her goddaughter would be arrested by my giving you fleeting assistance, you cannot know her well."

He had divined Lady Wolcot's intentions so well, she felt embarrassed for Imogen and looked away. Only his shiny Hessian boots remained in her line of vision.

A moment later he said, "Speaking of Miss Geddes, what is her reaction to the accusation?"

"She did not, of course, believe a word of it, except . . ." When his eyebrows rose a fraction, she went on in a much smaller voice, "This morning I bought myself a shawl, which is a rare indulgence for me. It is possible she began to wonder where I had obtained the money."

"Do you not earn a salary in Sir Donald's employ?"

She nodded. "But everyone who is acquainted with me knows I am a nipcheese and will not spend a penny more than I need."

The viscount laughed again. "Miss D'Arblay, I have encountered a number of clutch purses in my life, but you certainly do not sit well in their ranks, I assure you."

"Oh, it is not a natural quality, you understand. I was hoping eventually to be able to purchase my brother a commission. . . ."

Her voice tailed away when she came to realize this dream was now unattainable, and it was at this moment Lady Betteridge returned to the drawing room. Now she was accompanied by a tall, thin gentleman who had a distinguished appearance. He could not compare to Lord Trenton in elegance, but neither was he dandified like Foster Stanway and his cronies.

"Robert!" he greeted the viscount with genuine pleasure. "You look to be in plump currant, I see."

"Indeed, it is good to see you Arthur," the viscount responded with equal warmth.

How much more pleasant the atmosphere was in this house than in Lady Wolcot's, Serafina found herself reflecting.

"And you must be Miss D'Arblay," Sir Arthur said, turning to her, his smile fading somewhat.

Serafina had gotten to her feet and now she curtsied. "I am indeed, sir."

"I do believe you are just what I need."

"Sir?" she responded, feeling rather foolish.

"My wife tells me you are an archivist of some experience."

"Yes, sir. I last worked at Sir Donald Geddes's library at Coverdale."

"Bumpy Geddes? Well, if that doesn't beat the Dutch! I remember him well from our Cambridge days. We were commissioned into the same regiment, too! Now, Miss D'Arblay, Mira also tells me you are not presently employed."

For the first time in that ghastly afternoon Serafina actually laughed. "That is certainly true, sir."

"Excellent."

"How is that possible, sir?"

"Would you consider working for me?"

Serafina shook her head in bewilderment. "I could not . . ."

"I possess family documents which go back to the time of Elizabeth, and the library is overflowing with books that are in dire need of putting in some kind of order. It is beyond me. I can never find anything I want. I own it is often most frustrating. Is that not so, dear?"

Lady Betteridge nodded her agreement. "My husband gets himself into such a pelter about it. You would do us such a service, Miss D'Arblay, by accepting. We, of course, regret your misfortune, but it does seem as if you were fated to come to our rescue at this time. I knew it the moment it was mentioned, and I daresay your taking up this position will serve all our needs."

Serafina could not stop herself from looking to

Lord Trenton, who immediately said, "You might not feel yourself suited to being a paid companion, ma'am, but as my sister has said, this surely is the ideal solution to your present problem."

When Serafina looked at Sir Arthur, she asked, "Has Lady Betteridge made mention of the reason why I have no position at present, sir?"

"She mentioned some tarradiddle about Lady Wolcot's snuffboxes."

"And does that not bear any weight with you?"

Sir Arthur clucked his tongue with impatience. "It is patently evident to me that any female as sensible as you appear to be would not be so addle-pated to steal those gewgaws. You couldn't hope to get away with such a crime. It seems to me that her ladyship has put the saddle on the wrong horse on this occasion."

Just then Serafina could have kissed him, but she remained restrained. "Your proposition is certainly tempting, but if I do accept . . ."

"Please do," Lady Betteridge urged.

"It might become difficult for you. . . ."

Sir Arthur frowned. "Difficult? I think not. There might be occasions when you are working in the library and I get in your way somewhat, but . . ."

Serafina smiled again as Lord Trenton gently explained, "I don't believe Miss D'Arblay meant exactly that, Arthur."

The older man waved one hand in the air. "I shall pay you ten guineas more a year than your last employer. Does that sway you, my dear?"

"I'd accept if I were you," the viscount urged.

When she looked at him, her eyes met his. The

look that passed between them seemed to last forever, leaving her feeling almost as disturbed as she had been when she left her cousin's house, but for a very different reason.

"It is getting rather late," Lady Betteridge pointed out hastily when Serafina continued to hesitate. "Mayhap you would care to stay for dinner, Miss D'Arblay, and think on the matter tonight. You are welcome to stay here for the night so you may decide what you wish to do at leisure."

"How kind of you," Serafina murmured, almost overcome by their consideration and near to tears once again.

"Naturally, if you decide you will be too distressed by staying in London, then we will understand," her ladyship ventured.

Her words seemed suddenly to galvanize Serafina at last. "No, I shall not mind staying in London. The accusation remains a serious one wherever I reside, and I can only hope for a miracle which will, in due course, prove my innocence. I thank you, Sir Arthur, most humbly, and I accept your kind offer with gratitude and assure you I shall endeavor to give satisfaction."

Smiling now, Lady Betteridge started toward the door. "I shall go immediately and give instructions for a room to be made ready for you. A guest room overlooking the garden, I think . . ."

Her brother started after her. "And I shall have your boxes brought in," he told her as he strode across the room, the tassels on his Hessians swinging as he moved.

Just as he was about to pass her, she said shyly,

"I owe you a great debt of gratitude, my lord." The handkerchief he had pressed on to her was still in her hands, and she proffered the crumpled object with some embarrassment. "I seem to have creased it," she added, feeling quite foolish now.

He looked at it for a moment before taking it from her. "I doubt if you will from now on have recourse to tears," he said as he left the room.

"Now that that is settled, allow me to show you the library," Sir Arthur invited.

"Oh indeed," Serafina answered eagerly.

"I warn you it is not a small task I have charged you with, my dear."

"That will suit me perfectly, sir, for it will divert my mind from my odious situation."

She still felt somewhat bewildered, so suddenly had her fortunes changed yet again. She just hoped she would not, after all, regret staying in close proximity to Lady Wolcot, but she was even more acutely aware that by accepting Sir Arthur's excellent offer of employment, she would be in a position to see Lord Trenton at frequent intervals.

Serafina wondered if she would come to regret that, too.

# EIGHT

Despite all her initial misgivings, Serafina soon settled in to her task. Because she spent most of her day in the library, she saw little of any member of the family except at dinner whenever Sir Arthur and Lady Betteridge were at home, which wasn't all that often as they were a socially prominent couple. However, her ladyship had insisted, from the outset, that Serafina dine with them and had allocated her a spacious bedchamber of her own in direct contrast to the tiny garret she had occupied at Wolcot House.

Because Serafina felt that the *ton* must know of Lady Wolcot's accusation, she was not at all happy to mix with Lady Betteridge's dinner guests, but after being pressed to do so, she had found them without exception charming and attentive and eager to converse with her about her work in Sir Arthur's library.

It came as a considerable relief to her that Lord Trenton did not often call in at Betteridge House, at least not when she was aware of it. Her relief immediately led to a feeling of guilt, for he had been so kind in her hour of need, instrumental in finding a solution to her problem.

Serafina's enjoyment of her work in Sir Arthur's library almost made her forget the awful cloud of suspicion she felt was suspended over her. She spent long hours cataloging fascinating documents pertaining to the Betteridge family. Sometimes Sir Arthur joined her, and they enjoyed long conversations on the various categories of books, of which there were many.

If it were not for the matters that plagued her, Serafina felt she could have been very happy indeed, but she constantly fretted about being branded a thief and about Imogen's future. Not that it should have concerned her except that it involved Jolyon, and she was concerned about him, too.

One evening after Lady Betteridge had prevailed upon Serafina to play the pianoforte for them, her ladyship said, "You do everything so well, Miss D'Arblay, I feel we have very good value in you."

Serafina smiled shyly. She had only agreed to play because it was one of the rare evenings the Betteridge's had not dined out or had a number of invited guests themselves.

"I assure you it is I who is the more fortunate."

"Ah well, let us say we are all well suited. It is so pleasant to spend a quiet evening at home for once."

"It is a wonder all the hurry-scurry you involve yourself in doesn't overset your nerves," her husband pointed out, not unkindly.

"The Trentons are always strong, which is as well. Fortunately all is in readiness for our rout on the morrow. I fear it is going to be quite a hurricane!"

Serafina looked up from her sewing in alarm. "Oh, I had quite forgotten you were holding a rout, my lady."

"As I recall you were invited." She shook her head smilingly. "In all conscience I cannot conceive why I invited the Wolcot party. I do not usually include them on my guest list."

Serafina bit her lip. "Mayhap Lord Trenton asked it of you, ma'am."

Her ladyship smiled. "Ah yes, it is quite possible."

For a moment she stared strangely at Serafina in a considering manner, and then her husband said, refilling his glass with port, "I cannot abide that Wolcot woman. Never could. Lord Wolcot was a decent enough chap. Belonged to all the clubs. Pity he was petticoat led. That woman is nothing but a vulgar fussock, if you ask my opinion."

His wife laughed in some embarrassment. "Arthur dear, there is no need to speak so bluntly in front of Miss D'Arblay."

"Tush! If anyone has a derogatory opinion of Lady Wolcot it must be Miss D'Arblay. If Trenton is considering the Geddes chit as a match, he'd best consider the godmother, too. Wouldn't fancy her in the family. Not at all."

Lady Betteridge cast an apologetic look in the direction of Serafina, who was affecting not to listen. "I am persuaded my brother will weigh all considerations before making an offer to any female."

Serafina cleared her throat before venturing,

"Forgive me for asking, my lady, but as you are aware, Miss Geddes is dear to me, and it would be of the greatest interest to know if it is true that his lordship is in search of a wife."

"In all truth, my dear, I believe he would have settled a long time ago had he met his match."

"Surely it cannot be too difficult for a gentleman in Lord Trenton's position."

"Naturally, there have been many who would have been glad enough to marry him, and the same is still true. . . ."

"Too choosy, that's Trenton," Sir Arthur observed. "It is well past the time he should have hung up his ladle."

Ignoring her husband's observations, Lady Betteridge addressed Serafina once more, "I do hope you have a fetching gown to wear to our rout, my dear."

Once again Serafina started. "Me, my lady?"

Lady Betteridge looked amused. "Naturally. Your name, I recall, was included on the invitation. I'll wager you will be obliged to sit out very few sets, and an evening of this kind will be diverting for you. Let no one say you do not need a diversion."

Serafina shook her head, her eyes wide with fear. "Forgive me, my lady, but I couldn't possibly attend the rout."

"You need not concern yourself that *I* shall subject you to a setdown if you stand up to dance."

Serafina was bound to smile as she pointed out, "Lady Wolcot will be attending your rout, and she is sure to cause a kickup if she catches sight of me there. Such an unpleasant possibility is entirely avoidable."

"Come now, Mira," her husband chided, "not everyone enjoys such squeezes, you know."

"You do not, that much is always clear to me." Then she turned once again to Serafina. "Very well, I understand your reluctance. It was cork-brained of me not to consider it before. One can only hope the matter is soon cleared up for you cannot hide away forever."

"It is just as well I am not normally called up to mix in elevated company, or, more importantly, gatherings where Lady Wolcot will be present."

Much as Serafina dreaded coming face-to-face with the countess and indeed any of her cronies, she was just as reluctant to stand by and watch Lord Trenton pay court to Imogen, which was entirely for her brother's sake.

For the entire day preceding the rout, the Betteridge servants scurried to and fro, preparing rooms for the evening's diversion. What seemed to be hundreds of flowers were delivered and arranged in all of the rooms being used that evening. The kitchen was in chaos after the immense amount of food had begun to arrive, but when the time came for the rout to begin, all was in readiness, and Lady Betteridge looked serene in blue satin with an overskirt of silver net.

Serafina could not help but say, "You look breathtaking, my lady."

The woman smiled. "It is kind of you to say so. The sentiment is much appreciated, but I hope you will not spend the entire evening in the dismals."

"I assure you I will not, my lady."

When the first carriages began to rumble into the drive, Serafina, along with several of the housemaids retired to the upper landing from which they could observe the arrivals. Much comment was bandied about the fashions, most of which were impressive, although others were ludicrous and elicited a good deal of laughter. A king's ransom in fur cloaks alone was deposited with the footmen. Most of the gentlemen contrived to look quite elegant in evening dress, apart from those who were too stout. Sir Arthur and Lady Betteridge greeted everyone warmly, and Serafina held her breath a little when Lady Wolcot arrived with Imogen in tow.

Serafina thought her friend looked a little apprehensive but nonetheless beautiful in pink sarcenet with pearls at her throat and in her hair. Lady Wolcot as usual wore far too many of her jewels, but other ladies present had made a similar mistake so she did not look out of place.

Again Serafina found herself holding her breath when Lord Trenton arrived. As she had observed at Caroline's soiree, he looked extremely elegant in a dark blue evening coat which was excellently tailored, his neck cloth perfectly folded and pristine in its whiteness.

The housemaids immediately began to giggle and chatter among themselves when he had come into the hall. For once Serafina kept herself aloof from their comments that flattered the viscount. He dallied in the hall for some time, conversing with one acquaintance or another. However, he was just about to go into the ballroom, when he looked up as if he was suddenly aware of being observed, and Serafina stepped back out of view.

Later, when she heard the music drifting upward, she wondered who he might be dancing with and naturally presumed Imogen would be one of his partners during the evening. Perhaps not just once. If that was so, no one present would be left in any doubt about where he had fixed his interest.

Her cheeks grew hot at the realization that had she attended the rout, he would have asked her to stand up with him at some point during the evening. Lady Wolcot's wrath in that event would have been awful to contemplate, and Serafina was more than ever glad she had resisted the temptation to attend.

Unable to settle down to read in her room as she had intended, Serafina wandered into the music room, which was one of the few parts of the house empty of guests, and as the orchestra struck up a country dance she began to trace the steps on her own. At Coverdale she had shared dancing lessons with Imogen for a while and had even learned the steps of the new sensation, the waltz, which Imogen would not be allowed to participate in until her come-out.

A noise in the doorway made her start and look round in alarm to see the viscount standing there, a glass of champagne in each hand. She had no way of knowing how long he had been standing there, watching her, but she suspected it had been for some time, and her cheeks flushed with embarrassment.

However, he made no mention of her solitary dance. He just came farther into the room, holding out one of the glasses.

"When I discovered you were not present downstairs, I thought you might enjoy a glass of champagne all the same."

Serafina smiled shyly as he handed it to her. She looked away from him in great confusion. "How kind you are. You should not have troubled yourself."

"It is no trouble, I assure you, ma'am. The respite is welcome. It is devilishly hot down there."

She laughed self-consciously, and a moment later he held up his glass. "Let us make a toast to the truth, Miss D'Arblay. May it always be discovered."

As she sipped at the drink, she felt it immediately go to her head. "How it may be uncovered I have no notion."

He moved away from her, which was a great relief. He sat down on the pianoforte stool, his back to the instrument. "From what you have told me all the missing items are of great value."

"I believe only the most valuable of the snuffboxes are missing, but it makes no odds. Even if one of the least valuable were missing, the finger of accusation would still point in my direction."

"It does make a difference, ma'am. Such items are not easy to dispose of, if indeed that is why they were taken. No one could retain them for their own use, so . . ."

"It never occurred to Lady Wolcot that in the time that elapsed between the robbery taking place and its discovery, a greenhorn like myself would have had no method of disposing of the snuffboxes."

He smiled wryly. "I think you will agree that Lady Wolcot does not possess a great degree of intellectual prowess. I have made one or two inquiries. . . ." She looked at him in surprise. "And no one has been approached to buy snuffboxes, as far as I can ascertain."

"You are kind to trouble yourself, my lord, but . . ." She sighed, turning away. "I fear it is a hopeless task, akin to barking at the moon."

"I am not so easily discouraged, nor should you be. Where is that spark of spirit I believe I detected in you?"

In some embarrassment she gulped down the champagne. "I have no spirit. I am just striving to survive."

"I do not agree with you. Someone with less spirit would have been content to live on her aunt's charity."

The champagne had imbued her with a certain boldness, and she countered, "I cannot conceive why you should trouble yourself on my behalf."

He gave her a strange smile. "Let us just say I have a vested interest."

Imogen, she thought. He's doing it to impress Imogen. The fact that the girl's heart belonged to another would only serve to encourage him to strive harder. She wished she had thought about that before telling him. It must have been akin to throwing down a challenge. Imogen's heart would be his whatever he had to do to win it.

She turned to look at him again. "Have you, by any chance, spoken to Imogen this evening?"

"At some length, you'll be glad to learn. However, I feel bound to say she is quite distraught about you."

"Poor Imogen. I was afraid this botheration would prey on her mind. I feel so dreadful about not being with her at the very time she needs me most."

He drained his own champagne glass before saying, "Miss Geddes will survive."

"Yes, I know she will, but all the same . . ."

"And so will you, Miss D'Arblay."

Serafina turned to him again, betraying a little concern. "Did you tell her I was living here?"

"I gathered you did not wish it to be known."

"Yes, that is so. I am obliged to you for not mentioning it."

"Personally, I am bound to say I believe that to be a mistake."

"Oh? I cannot conceive why you should think so."

"Whoever has stolen those snuffboxes can rest happy now that you are believed to be the culprit and banished for good to the country." He paused for a moment before adding in a carefully considered manner, "If, however, it was known you were still in town, the miscreant might rest a little less easy. But it is entirely up to you if you wish to continue playing least in sight. I do not agree with it. However, I do understand your wish for anonymity, which I believe is coupled with a laudable desire to protect my sister from any unpleasant gossip ensuing from your presence in her house."

He got to his feet and put the glass down on a nearby table just as the music for a waltz struck up in the ballroom downstairs. Serafina thought he was about to take his leave of her, and she was considering carefully all he had said when he stopped and turned on his heel.

"Do you dance the waltz, Miss D'Arblay?"

"I learned with Imogen at Coverdale," she answered, somewhat startled.

"If you cannot come down to the ballroom and dance, will you do me the honor of standing up with me here?"

Serafina could not help but laugh. "You are roasting me, I fear, my lord."

He came toward her, taking the empty glass from her yielding fingers and placing it on a drum table. Then, with no further ado, he took her in his arms and began to dance.

Serafina had never been held so close to any man before and froze momentarily. A moment later, though, she began to follow his steps just as she had been taught to do. At the time she had never imagined she would be called upon to partner someone, to be held so close to a gentleman. No wonder the dance's introduction had caused such a sensation in society. She had been quite content to stand on the sidelines and watch others participate in this, the most intimate of dances yet invented.

To Serafina it was as if she was in the grip of a fantastic dream, and all too soon the music came to an end, but he did not relinquish his hold on her immediately. The champagne must have affected her considerably, for Serafina felt quite lightheaded, not to mention lighthearted now, but as her eyes met his, she saw something in them that made her heart flutter unevenly.

At last the sound of laughter caused him to relinquish his hold on her, and she moved quickly away from him, averting her face. She was aware that the people in the doorway, a little the worse for drink it appeared, were looking at her curiously, no doubt wondering who she might be.

Serafina lowered her eyes demurely as Lord Trenton bowed and walked out of the room, taking the revelers with him. When quietness prevailed again, the music having receded into the background of her mind, she sat down on the piano stool and stared ahead of her, not seeing anything but experiencing emotions that were entirely new to her.

What she finally came to understand was that she was dangerously attracted to a man who could never be hers.

# NINE

"Miss D'Arblay, there is a gentleman wishing to see you waiting without."

Serafina had been hard at work, and she looked up uncomprehendingly at the footman. "To see me?"

"Yes, ma'am. He asked for you by name."

She sat back in her chair, frowning, worried, for no one apart from Lord Trenton, Sir Arthur, and Lady Betteridge knew she was here, and a feeling of dread began to pervade her heart.

The footman was holding out a silver tray bearing a solitary calling card that she belatedly noticed. Reluctantly she took it and then gasped, "Jolyon! How is it possible?"

"Would you have me show him in, ma'am?"

"Oh, please do!"

As the lackey went to do her bidding, Serafina's thoughts milled around in her head, and then she pushed back the chair and hurried to the library door just as a young man in a brown riding coat and buff pantaloons was shown in.

"Jolyon!" she cried, questions crowded out by the sheer joy of seeing him so unexpectedly.

She hugged him to her, and when she stood back, he carefully straightened his neck cloth. As he did so, he glanced around him, gasping, "My stars! Did you ever see such a large library in town?"

"It's magnificent, isn't it? Sir Arthur is quite a collector. Now, Joly, just what are you doing here in London?"

"I might just as well ask what you are doing *here.* I've been involved in a wild-goose chase all afternoon. I was beginning to get into a pucker about finding you at all."

"Come and sit by me," she invited, "and I will explain, but just how did you find me?"

As she led him to a chair, he answered, "Naturally, my first call was at Manchester Square, where I was told in no uncertain terms that you were no longer in residence. Then I had no option but to call in at Cousin Wallace's house and was dismayed to discover you were not there either. Fortunately some footman fellow told me that a Lord Trenton's tiger had collected your boxes and I should try here. In both houses I am bound to say I was as welcome as water in the shoes. What on earth is going on, Sal? I have never heard of Sir Arthur and Lady Betteridge, or indeed Lord Trenton. Why are you here and not with Imogen at Lady Wolcot's house?"

"First be pleased to tell me what you are doing in London, when I believed you to be in the country where I left you with Aunt Wyndham."

The young man looked suddenly shamefaced. "I couldn't stay there, Sal, and that's the truth of it. I was in a constant fidge, thinking of Imogen being so far away, being paid court to by some pink of the *ton*, or man-milliner. It had got to the stage I could think of little else, and it was becoming well-nigh unbearable."

"We discussed this at length, dearest, before Imogen and I left for London, as I recall. There is naught you can do save perhaps bark at the moon. Imogen is bound for an elevated marriage, just as she has always been, and you know it as well as I do."

The young man's face grew tense as he stared past Serafina into space. "I know it all right, but I have no intention of making it easy for her to settle for another man. She threw her cap over the windmill for me and none other. . . ."

"Calf love, Joly," she reminded him gently.

"I don't hold with that," he snapped.

"Oh, Joly, dearest, you must accept the situation."

"Imogen has no more wish to become a debutante and marry a tulip of fashion than you, Sal. She has just had her pretty little head turned by her mama and that godmother of hers. It is all for their glory not hers."

"I don't doubt there is a little truth in what you say, dearest, but Imogen is to make her debut, and from all I have witnessed so far, she will have no difficulty in finding a score of eligible suitors."

"Imogen might well end up riveted to a royal duke, but I have made up my mind that she will be obliged to conduct her flirting in my presence."

His sister smiled at him sympathetically. "What

difference will that make, save to distress you even further?"

"If I'd stayed at Wyndham House, she could easily put me out of her mind. She might even forget me entirely, but if I am here, she can't do it so easily, don't you see?"

Serafina was tempted to tell him not to be so foolish, but she belatedly recalled that the viscount had made a similar observation about her own situation, and she hesitated.

"Perchance it is not so foolish a notion after all," she murmured at last, and he brightened up considerably.

"It's plucky of you to say so, Sal. I thought you'd ring a peal over me when you saw me." He frowned then. "Now tell me why you aren't looking after Imogen as you are supposed to be doing?"

Serafina drew in a deep sigh. She knew, naturally, she could not delay in telling him, for if he was to remain in London, he was likely to hear about it soon enough. As quickly and as briefly as possible she related the sad tale of her dismissal by Lady Wolcot to her brother, whose expression veered between incredulity and anger.

When she had finished, he cried, "Flesh and fire! What balderdash! You a loose screw? Did her ladyship not attempt to discover the true culprit before she accused you?"

"As far as I am aware, she was quite convinced she had found her. There was no point in inquiring further."

"In my opinion it's deuced havey-cavey. You didn't go there to have your comb cut. She shouldn't be allowed to escape the consequences of giving you Turkish treatment. There is only one thing for it! She will have to be made to apologize to you."

Serafina could not help but laugh. "No, she will not." In a more gentle manner, she added, "You have not had the dubious honor of making her ladyship's acquaintance."

"I intend to do so with no further delay, I assure you, and have no fear she will receive the most severe wigging from me."

"No, no, you must not stir up the coals on my behalf, dearest. Lady Wolcot believes herself to be in the right in this matter, and there is naught you can do to change her mind, I fear. If you have any sense at all, Joly, you will keep away from her as much as possible. Lady Wolcot can more than hold her own in a kickup, and there is no sense in your crossing swords with her. Think of Imogen. She would be put in a most invidious position."

"It's a ramshackle business and no mistake," the young man admitted a moment later.

"I do agree."

"For all that has happened, you appear in great spout, I am delighted to observe."

"Why should I not be? Sir Arthur and Lady Betteridge have made me very welcome indeed. I could so easily have been thrown into Newgate, you know."

"Balderdash! Why did you not go to Cousin Wyndham when this happened?"

"I did, but his counsel was for me to go back to Coverdale. He thought I would be an embarrassment to him if I remained."

"He always was a Jack Straw, but mayhap you should have gone back, Sal. For once Cousin Wyndham might have been correct."

"How could I have gone back, Joly, with the accusation of theft hanging over me? It would have been as good as an admission of guilt."

He smiled then. "You always were as proud as an apothecary. Well, I can at least thank this Lord Trenton for his assistance to you. It is the least I can do."

He was already beginning to get to his feet, and Serafina said quickly, "Before you do anything of the kind, I feel I must tell you his lordship is one of Imogen's most favored suitors."

The young man thumped his clenched fist down on the arm of the chair. "Wouldn't you know it? He sounds a splendid fellow, but I declare he will never love Imogen as much as I do."

"I don't suppose he will, but he is rich and titled, and mayhap Imogen prefers those qualities to the ones you possess."

Jolyon smiled mirthlessly. "I only possess qualities like poverty. I can't even afford to dress like a nonpareil. I am bound to confess I feel totally dispirited."

"You look fine," she assured him. "Where are you staying?"

"Some chums of mine from Oxford are lodging in Dean Street, so I've joined them there. Sal, I really need to see Imogen."

"I do beg you to be careful with her, Joly," she warned. "Of late Imogen has had her head turned at every quarter."

"I can't credit that! It sounds like a high flyer to me."

"Joly, I am not bamming you. If you blunder in on her now, it might just have the opposite effect to the one you want."

"You are always full of good sense, but I might as well try to put a hat on a hen as stay away from her."

"I do not counsel you to do that."

He looked at her with interest. "What do you suggest I do?"

"Imogen has a busy social calendar, even now before the Season begins when she makes her official debut. Lady Wolcot informed me that most alliances are contracted before the Season begins, and I have no reason to doubt that. It won't be in the least difficult for you to encounter Imogen around town, but do try to curb your ardor, dearest. Try to be casual, however hard that might be."

"No doubt about that," the young man answered, laughing harshly.

"It might be best if you try to make it appear you are here for your own pleasure and not because of her. It might make all the difference to her attitude if she believes you are hanging out for a wife and not wearing the willow for her."

He nodded thoughtfully. "I get your drift, Sal. You have plenty of rumgumption."

She smiled fondly at him. "Wonderful as it is for me to see you here, dearest, I do have work to do, and plenty of it as you can see."

He looked all at once serious. "One day I vow I

shall be able to support you in the manner you deserve."

As she walked with him to the door, she replied, "We have contrived well so far, Joly, and I daresay we shall continue to do so."

"That is not good enough for you, in my opinion, Sal. You deserve the very best of everything, which is more than Aunt Wyndham ever gave you."

"Aunt Wyndham did well enough for us."

"Grudgingly, like her nipcheese of a son. They could have given you a Season and the chance of contracting a good marriage."

"I didn't want a Season," she replied, thinking wistfully of Lord Trenton.

When they reached the hall and Serafina and her brother were taking farewell of each other, Lady Betteridge came hurrying in, returning from her afternoon calls. She looked taken aback to find Serafina with a visitor, a male one at that.

"My lady, allow me to introduce my brother, Jolyon D'Arblay," Serafina said quickly.

As the young man bowed low before her, Lady Betteridge said, "Miss D'Arblay has made mention of you often, sir. I am delighted to make your acquaintance."

"It is my honor entirely, my lady, and as the head of my family, I should like to express my deepest gratitude for your kindness toward my sister."

Her ladyship's lips twitched slightly, but her demeanor remained attentive. "It is kind of you to express such sentiments, sir, but it is not necessary, I assure you. Miss D'Arblay more than earns her keep here. My husband is well pleased with her work. Are you newly arrived in London?"

"Yes, my lady."

"Do you intend to stay here for long?"

"I cannot be sure but certainly for the present, my lady."

"Mayhap you would care to stay for tea?" She glanced inquiringly at Serafina.

It was her brother who replied, "It is kind of you to ask, my lady, but I have business to attend to, and I believe I have kept Serafina from her work sufficiently long."

"You must feel free to call upon your sister as often as you wish."

"That is excessively civil of you, my lady," the young man replied, glancing delightedly at his sister.

"I am most obliged, my lady," Serafina added.

Lady Betteridge looked suddenly thoughtful. "As you have only recently arrived, I daresay you have not as yet contracted many social engagements."

"That is certainly true, my lady."

"Then mayhap you might wish to join us when we visit Vauxhall Gardens on the morrow. It is quite a diverting place, especially for a young man about town. If you do agree to joining us, I daresay Miss D'Arblay will come along, too, and that will be no bad thing, for she has scarce been out of the house since she arrived."

He glanced at Serafina inquiringly. "Will you go, Sal?"

"Oh, I think not," she replied, sounding regretful, "but *you* must, dearest."

"Not without you," he insisted, glancing at her ladyship.

"Your brother is quite correct, Miss D'Arblay. You should not hide away. You have no cause. Do come with us. It is certain to divert your mind."

"How can I refuse?" she conceded at last, smiling at them both, still with some uncertainty.

Jolyon took Lady Betteridge's hand and raised it to his lips. "Until the morrow, ladies."

Lady Betteridge watched him go, a smile on her lips. "I don't doubt his presence in London will cause many a female heart to flutter."

"I do hope you are correct, my lady, for it might divert *his* mind and salve his wounded pride if other young ladies set their caps at him. He might no longer wear the willow for Imogen."

Belatedly recalling that her ladyship's brother was in earnest over Imogen, Serafina quickly excused herself and hurried back to her work in the library.

# TEN

By the time the Betteridge party was ready to leave for Vauxhall Gardens the following evening, Serafina regretted her impulsive agreement to go, which was purely an act of cowardice on her part. From all she had heard of the pleasure gardens, she was curious to see it for herself and being included in Sir Arthur and Lady Betteridge's party was an honor indeed. Serafina told herself she owed it to Jolyon to help him become as socially successful as possible. He had looks and address. All he lacked was a fortune, but for a good-looking young man, that was not quite as tragic as it was for a female.

After agonizing for a long time, Serafina finally decided to wear her blue-velvet gown. She had always considered it becoming, but since her arrival in London, seeing guests at Betteridge House, she had come to accept how dowdy it really was. But it made no odds, as it was the only gown she possessed that suited the purpose.

Lady Betteridge kindly pronounced her charming when Serafina joined them for dinner preceding their departure for Vauxhall. She smiled her gratitude and glanced around the drawing room furtively, not knowing whether she was relieved or disappointed that the viscount wasn't there. She always felt so confused when she thought about him, recalling often their dance together in the music room and the way he had spoken to her on their first encounter. Fortunately her intense concentration upon her work ensured she could occasionally put out of her mind what were unwelcome memories.

Jolyon arrived promptly after dinner, wearing an evening coat of exquisite tailoring that would have done justice to Beau Brummell himself. Serafina could not help but stare in astonishment at her brother, who was suddenly an elegant young man.

"I don't suppose you have attended Vauxhall Gardens before," Sir Arthur inquired of him.

"No, sir, and I confess to be looking forward to the experience with great relish." He glanced at his sister. "I don't doubt that Serafina will also enjoy the diversion."

"Your sister," Lady Betteridge replied, looking at her wryly, "has earned her respite."

"I do not for one moment doubt it, my lady," Jolyon replied, and Serafina found her cheeks going pink.

The carriage to which they were ushered was to be shared with Sir Arthur's rather deaf aunt, so Serafina was able to ask as soon as they set off, "How did you come by that coat, Joly?"

"Elegant, ain't it?" he answered, smugly touching his carefully folded neck cloth.

"Undoubtedly," she snapped. "I suppose it was shockingly expensive, too."

"The best does not come cheap, and it is my understanding that Stulz is the best tailor in London."

"There are those who would argue in favor of Weston," she replied sarcastically. "But what is pertinent is how you contrived to pay for it. I do hope you are not emulating the example of some bucks who run up large bills with tradesmen. They usually have expectations."

"I am not such a gudgeon, Sal. I won a wager."

Serafina looked at him aghast. "Jolyon! You know full well you cannot afford to game deep."

"I didn't. It was just a small wager between Tom and Freddy and I. They're the chums with whom I lodge." He laughed at the recollection while his sister stared at him coldly. "We made a wager on what color coat Piggy Benton would be wearing when he turned up for dinner at Watiers the other evening."

As Serafina gasped with annoyance at such irresponsible behavior, Jolyon went on, smiling at the dowager facing him, "Next time I find myself plump in the pocket, I intend to buy you the finest, most modish, gown there is. And a bonnet with the longest feather in it to match. Oh yes, and you shall have a fur tippet. Ermine no less."

"No, Jolyon. I do not want you to buy me anything of the kind, and I beseech you not to gamble again, for you cannot afford to lose."

"Oh, come now, dearest, don't get into a pelter about it, for it is only chicken stakes. I can pay my shot, you know. Our trust is quite generous, especially as you have steadfastly refused to draw on it for years."

"I don't need more than I am able to earn."

"Yes, you do. You've always worn Aunt Wyndham's cast-off clothes, and they're outmoded when they're new."

"I don't give a straw for that."

"Well, you should. You could easily outdazzle everyone if you had the correct clothes. You wouldn't be the first pauper to marry a fortune, if you put your mind to it."

"Jolyon, I am almost out of patience with you. You are talking such humbug I cannot bear to listen."

He turned to look at her in the half-light shed by the torches born by the linkboys running beside the carriage. "Serafina," he said, using her full name, which was unusual, "don't you know how I hate to see you like this, even when you are employed by congenial people like Sir Arthur and Lady Betteridge? You could just as well find yourself with another Lady Wolcot next time. I can't bear to think of it."

"You mustn't concern yourself with me, Joly. There really wouldn't be any point in my outdazzling anyone, would there?"

He drew a sigh and sank back into the squabs. "I saw Foster Stanway the other evening at Brooks's."

Although she was relieved at the change of subject, Serafina looked at him curiously, uneasy at the mention of that man's name. Anyone connected with the odious Lady Wolcot caused her great discomfort.

"Did you speak of me?"

"Good grief no! I don't suppose he has any notion we are related as yet, but as I have no intention of hiding our kinship, he will know it soon enough. He must be full of juice, for he games deep, unless, of course, her ladyship keeps him in funds."

"It's possible. She adores him, although I cannot conceive why, apart from his endless flattery."

"He believes himself to be right up to the knocker, but I consider him a court card. Do you think Imogen will be at Vauxhall tonight?" he asked a moment later.

"It's entirely possible. Lady Betteridge gave me to understand it's a special gala evening, and the *ton* will attend in great numbers."

"I confess to being most disappointed not to have set eyes upon her since I arrived. This afternoon I hired a hack from Tilbury and rode the Grant Strut in Hyde Park in the hope of catching sight of her, to no avail."

"Patience will prevail, dearest," Serafina replied, patting him comfortingly on the arm. "But do remember what I told you yesterday: behave charmingly to as many other young ladies as you are able, and do not act the mooncalf in front of Imogen."

Jolyon did not appear entirely convinced of that stategy, for he replied, "I do trust you are correct in what you counsel, Sal."

"Well, you did act in earnest when you were both at Coverdale, and it made no difference, so it's like you have nothing to lose."

"Mayhap she didn't believe I *was* in earnest."

The conversation was, of necessity, brought to an

end by their arrival at Vauxhall Gardens. Despite a very natural dread of encountering Lady Wolcot, Serafina did experience a thrill of excitement and wished she could have shared that with Imogen.

She was impressed by the long avenues of trees, lit by countless lanterns. It looked like a fairy grotto to Serafina, who was also happy to observe that should Lady Wolcot be present, it would be a simple matter to evade her along all the dark walks.

As the Betteridge party proceeded to their box in the rotunda, they passed pretty cascades and fountains that brought forth gasps of admiration. Some of the party paused to admire Roubilac's statue of Mr. Handel, the composer, which was held to be very lifelike.

At that moment Serafina felt certain she had been right in agreeing to come along. When they were settled into the box, it was to await the evening's main entertainment, which was said to be quite spectacular.

Most of the gentlemen, Jolyon included, did not care to wait in the box and immediately excused themselves to wander around until the entertainment actually began. Serafina was happy enough to watch the other boxes fill with a mainly aristocratic audience, some of whom she recalled seeing on other occasions, most of whom she did not.

"I heard the most monstrous thing today," Lady Randall confided in the other ladies.

One thing Serafina had learned during her stay in London: when ladies of the *ton* met together, it was to exchange all the latest *on-dits*. Gossip was an important part of their lives, and even the most innocuous occurrence was noted and commented upon repeatedly.

"Prinny has ordered—yes ordered—that the Princess Charlotte shall not live with Princess Caroline. How can he be allowed to escape the consequences of subjecting his wife and daughter to such Turkish treatment?"

"One supposes," Lady Betteridge replied in a wry manner, "that as Prince Regent, he can do as he pleases."

"It ain't just," another lady argued, and then smiling at her hostess added, "By the by, my lady, where is your charming brother this evening? His humor is so droll, I always enjoy his company."

Although Serafina was apparently watching the arrivals with rapt interest, she listened anxiously for her ladyship's answer.

"My brother had a prior engagement, although I daresay he enjoys your company, too, and regrets being absent from it this evening."

The lady played coyly with her fan. "I don't believe for one moment Lord Trenton will be missing any of us this evening. I know he prefers the company of Corinna Wilding."

Lady Betteridge smiled. "Who can blame him, ma'am? Not only is she the most vivacious of all the demireps, but half the gentlemen of the *ton* vie for her interest."

Lady Randall leaned forward, looking at Lady Betteridge with interest. "Mira, my dear, I have been meaning to inquire of you; who was the chit he was seen dancing with in your music room during the rout the other evening?"

"I have heard mention of it, too," Mrs. Granby added, looking at her hostess with interest. "Everyone is agog to know."

Serafina froze and kept up her appearance of not attending to the conversation, but she was aware that her ladyship was looking somewhat perplexed.

After a moment's hesitation she answered, "As I was engaged in dancing in the ballroom, I know nothing of the matter."

Her friends laughed in disbelief, and Lady Randall said, "Someone must know who it was."

"Lily Priest's chit, I don't doubt," Mrs. Granby suggested. "She is shameful enough for such an exploit. What a hoyden!"

"Until we know for certain it is Lizzie Priest, this has the makings of a great intrigue," Lady Randall added with a laugh.

"The simple solution is for you to ask my brother when next you see him," Lady Betteridge suggested, eliciting great laughter from all the ladies in the box.

Most of the other boxes had filled by now, and the gentlemen began to return.

Jolyon whispered to Serafina, "I have seen Imogen!"

The vexing conversation was immediately banished from her mind as she asked, "Did she see you?"

"Yes, I made certain of it, and I am bound to confess she expressed no pleasure in seeing me."

"Do not let it trouble your head, dearest. Your appearance must have been a shock to her and bound to disconcert her at first. Where is she? Do you know?"

"She was making her way with her party to a box. Look, Sal, over there to the left a little."

Lady Wolcot, who was overdressed and bejeweled, could not easily be missed. Fortunately Imogen looked as lovely as always and was smiling, which gave Serafina some crumb of comfort. Foster Stanway followed them into the box, but then Serafina gasped out loud when she caught sight of Lord Trenton in the party. He seated himself close to Imogen, to whom he kept addressing his remarks, which made her smile even more broadly.

Serafina was unable to take her eyes off them, until a very few minutes later the first act appeared on the stage, a lady who danced on a white, prancing horse.

When the act was over, both Serafina and Jolyon applauded enthusiastically, but Lady Betteridge declared she had seen better at Astley's Amphitheatre.

"If that is so, it must be a truly amazing place," Serafina gasped.

"You must come with us the next time we go and see for yourself," her ladyship told her.

The second act, Mrs. Franklin, a singer of great sensitivity brought forth more applause and found favor among the rather jaded audience in the Betteridge box. Ramo Samee, an Indian juggler, was the next act to hold them all in thrall, except for Serafina, who found her attention straying to Lady Wolcot's party, and Lord Trenton in particular.

By the time Mr. Mountain came on to sing some

sentimental tunes, Serafina had become convinced she had committed a grave error in coming to Vauxhall Gardens. Finally, Madame Saqui from Paris made everyone gasp with her tightrope-walking act.

After she had finished, it was Jolyon who declared: "I cannot recall when I have enjoyed myself more!"

"And you, Miss D'Arblay?" Sir Arthur inquired.

"It has been most diverting," she replied and became aware that Lady Betteridge was watching her with that odd, considering, look once again.

It gave Serafina something of a start to realize that her ladyship must be only too well aware of who had danced with her brother in the music room on the night of the rout, and it embarrassed her to think so innocent an act had resulted in so much gossip.

A moment later Lady Betteridge had reverted to her more usual vivacious self and suggested, "Let us adjourn to the supper box. I have no doubt we are all in need of a hearty supper before we join the dancing in the pavilion."

"What is amiss?" Jolyon asked as they walked through the crowds to the supper box. "You're as mute as a fish."

Serafina responded with a genuine smile. "Forgive me, dearest, but seeing Lady Wolcot merely reminded me of the invidious position in which I find myself."

"I wish there was something I could do to help prove your innocence, Sal. When it comes to anything of import, I am useless."

"You must not for anything think so. There is naught *anyone* can do, least of all you."

Suddenly, as they approached the supper box in the sylvan setting of a leafy arbor, Serafina caught sight of a wide-eyed Imogen pushing her way through the crowds to reach them.

"Serafina, I had no notion *you* were still in town. It was surprise enough to see Jolyon. Did you come up together?"

"I never left," Serafina answered in some embarrassment.

"Oh! I had no notion. Why did you not let me know?"

"I did not wish to cause you any further embarrassment."

"Tush! Such nonsense. Do you stay with Mr. and Mrs. Wyndham?"

"No, I do not."

"Then where . . . ?" the girl asked, looking bewildered, and Serafina regretted bitterly not being able to confide in her.

"Where I am residing is of no account." The girl looked wide-eyed from Jolyon to Serafina, who added, "If you need me, be certain I shall come to hear of it."

Imogen began to back away from them. "I must return to our party before I am missed. I was never more surprised. . . . Are you short of funds, Serafina? I do have some pin money by me if you need it."

Serafina smiled her thanks. "No, I am quite comfortable, you may be sure."

The girl looked suddenly wretched. "I just want

you to know, I never believed you guilty of theft," she said as she moved away.

"I shall see you later," Jolyon told her. His gaze had never left Imogen all the while she had conversed with his sister. "She agreed to stand up with me when I spoke to her earlier," he added when she had gone.

"Lady Wolcot will not like it. Do not be too persistent."

"I don't care a fig for what her ladyship does or does not like."

"Jolyon," Serafina said with some difficulty, "be exceedingly careful of Lady Wolcot. If she perceives you as a threat to her plans for Imogen, she might do you harm."

"Do me harm?" he echoed in some perplexity. "What do you mean by that?"

When she made no answer, he went on, "You cannot mean to intimate *she* might have engineered the loss of her own snuffboxes to get at you."

"I really cannot say for certain," Serafina answered in some embarrassment, "but it really is not beyond her. You see, Joly, I have come to understand that Lady Wolcot is not received in the drawing rooms of the *haute ton*, and I do suspect she hopes that if Imogen makes a truly brilliant marriage, that might well be her way of entry into elevated society."

"If that is only partly true, it is monstrous," Jolyon concluded. "In any event I have already won Imogen's heart. There is naught Lady Wolcot can do about it now."

"I do not doubt that for one moment, dearest, but

I assure you Lady Wolcot will not stand idly by and allow a penniless nobody to marry Imogen."

"We shall see," he vowed, causing his sister to feel even more uneasy.

When everyone was assembled inside the box, a simple supper of shaved ham, powdered beef, and rack punch was served, followed by a selection of syllabubs and custards. Everyone partook of the food with gusto except for Serafina, whose mind remained full of her conversation with Imogen.

Afterward everyone paired off, except for Sir Arthur's aunt, who went to admire the many floral displays in the gardens. Jolyon escorted his unenthusiastic sister toward the pavilion from which music floated invitingly along on the summer air.

"I really feel I ought to stay in the supper box," she ventured.

"That's a humbug, Sal. You decided quite rightly to stop hiding away from everyone. You cannot go back on that decision now."

"Why can I not?"

"Because I have no intention of allowing you to do so."

She smiled faintly. "I do wonder if it is a good notion, after all."

"You are innocent, are you not?"

"Of course!"

"Then hold up your head."

"I am so glad you are here, dearest," she told him in heartfelt tones, "even though I do fear for your happiness."

"Imogen's marriage to another would cause me unhappiness whether I am here or in Coverdale," he reasoned, as they joined the set being made up for a minuet.

Somehow Serafina knew exactly how he felt, and for the first time she experienced the pain of longing herself, but she refused to allow her thoughts to continue in that direction for long.

Just as the dance was about to begin, she froze when she caught sight of Lady Wolcot taking her place in the set with Foster Stanway. Her ladyship was at that moment unaware of Serafina's presence, but a moment later she saw her, and her expression quickly changed from one of benevolence to that of disbelief.

Fortunately, or perhaps not, Serafina's attention was diverted by the arrival of Imogen accompanied by Lord Trenton, who both took their places in the set. Imogen saw Serafina and Jolyon immediately, and her cheeks grew pink as she looked quickly away again. Lord Trenton noted his partner's discomfiture and then the reason for it. Just at that moment the dance began, and Serafina could not recall when she had ever disliked participating in a dance so heartily.

As partners changed in the course of the dance, Serafina soon found herself facing Foster Stanway, who smiled at her in what she considered to be an impudent manner. It was far more of an ordeal when she partnered Lord Trenton, whose dark eyes bore a look of silent amusement in them.

That puzzled her somewhat, but as the dance progressed, she came to understand that her situation did, no doubt, amuse him. Belatedly she recalled hearing tales of wealthy young bucks whose constant boredom prompted them to involve themselves in outrageous activities.

At that moment she came to suspect that Lord Trenton had come to her aid just to see how everyone would react to her company—Lady Wolcot's reaction when she came to know of her presence in London, how Serafina herself dealt with being suspected of theft, and her behavior in the presence of her accuser. Young men of his kind were guilty of far worse larks, as Foster Stanway had related when she first arrived in London. Lord Trenton might even have made wagers as to the final outcome of her shocking situation.

When the dance ended, Jolyon told her, "Imogen has promised the next set to me."

Serafina forced a smile to her lips. "I daresay that cannot be taken amiss."

"Will you contrive if I leave you for a short while?"

Now her indulgent smile was a genuine one. "Indeed I will. I believe I shall go to see the hermit who sits in a cave somewhere around the gardens. I shall see you back at the supper box presently. Go along quickly before you lose sight of her."

In urging Jolyon to go and seek out Imogen, she was disguising her own anxiety to leave the pavilion, reasoning that all those she wished to avoid would remain to enjoy the dancing. However, she had gone only a few paces when a familiar voice arrested her.

"Miss D'Arblay!" She turned on her heel to find herself facing an implacable Lady Wolcot. "When I clapped eyes upon you earlier, I was persuaded they must be deceiving me."

To hide her confusion Serafina dropped into a curtsy. "As you see, my lady, your eyes are exceedingly sharp."

"I believed you to be back at Coverdale by now."

"I regret I decided it was in my own best interest to remain here in town, my lady."

The countess's eyes narrowed. "Where exactly are you residing?"

"With friends, my lady," she answered truthfully.

Lady Wolcot's face began to grow red. "What is their name?"

"I am not at liberty to disclose that."

The countess stiffened, not troubling to hide her anger now. "Why do you remain in town, madam?"

"Because I wished to do so, my lady," Serafina answered with deceptive meekness.

Her words had the required effect, and Lady Wolcot's bosom began to heave. "How dare you be so insolent to me? Have you not injured me sufficiently?"

"If you would but believe me, my lady, I have not injured you at all."

"What humbug! You cannot possibly find a position here without a recommendation."

"Can I not?"

"And let me tell you, my girl, I have written to Lady Geddes to inform her of your perfidy."

"That does not surprise me in the least, but although you turned me out of your house, you have no authority whatsoever to run me out of *London*, my lady."

The countess's eyes almost stood out of their sockets. "Why you impudent baggage! I believe I have been acting with the utmost restraint in this matter, and I've a mind to call a constable even now."

"I believe you would need rather more proof against me than a mere suspicion."

Lady Wolcot was growing so angry Serafina suddenly suspected she might succumb to a seizure, but then her demeanor changed quite suddenly and dramatically.

"Why, Lady Wolcot, I have been seeking you out for an age." Serafina immediately recognized Lord Trenton's silky tones. "I would very much like the honor of standing up with you for the next set, if you are free."

He had come up unseen behind Serafina, who scarcely dared to glance at him. For his part he only subjected her to a brief, uninterested, glance.

"Gladly, my lord," the countess responded, looking flustered, as well she might. "This, can you comprehend, is the vile creature who stole my property."

The viscount cast Serafina a cool, appraising look, affecting a supercilious air that was most fashionable in the ranks of gentlemen of the *ton*.

"You do not look in the least like a loose screw, madam," he told her in so laconic a manner, she was obliged to bite her lip hard in an effort to suppress her laughter, and then as he offered his arm to the countess, he went on, "What I like about

Vauxhall Gardens, my lady, is the interesting mix of classes, including the criminal one."

"I have been most cruelly used by that young lady," Serafina heard the countess tell him.

"You must relate the whole sorry tale to me," he responded in a sympathetic manner.

As they strolled back toward the dance floor, Lord Trenton turned slightly and cast Serafina a mischievous look. Tremulously she returned the smile before making a delayed departure from the pavilion at last.

# ELEVEN

The library door closed so quietly, Serafina did not immediately realize someone had entered the room until she heard a footstep. She had been working intently on the second level of the library. When she became aware of another presence in the room, she walked to the balustrade, expecting to see Sir Arthur, who, in any event, had declared his intention of being absent from home for most of the day.

She certainly did not expect to see Lord Trenton, looking around him with interest, and she started nervously. Her movement must have become apparent to him, for he looked up.

"Ah, so there you are Miss D'Arblay. For a moment I thought the library must be empty."

"Sir Arthur is not at home," she ventured.

"So Dillon has informed me. I decided to stay nevertheless and inquire of you. How are you faring?"

"Very well indeed, I thank you," she answered in all truth, and then when he seemed inclined to linger, she went down the stairs to join him on the main floor of the library.

He glanced around at the thousands of books that

lined the walls on two levels. "I can see that Sir Arthur has given you a great task."

"For a woman?" she asked, dimpling.

"For anyone," he answered with a smile.

"It is a challenge, I own, but it is one I am relishing, I assure you, my lord."

His eyes met hers then. "Yes, Miss D'Arblay, I, too, enjoy a challenge."

Serafina shivered slightly and turned away from his disturbing gaze, although he still remained uncomfortably close. "I have reason to be obliged to you yet again, my lord."

"I cannot think why."

"The other evening at Vauxhall. I have a notion you came to rescue me from Lady Wolcot."

"Ah yes. You evidently discerned that Lady Wolcot was not a female I would normally be in a great fidge to engage for a dance, but you have no cause to be obliged to me, ma'am. Any man of sensibility would have come to your rescue in such circumstances, for it was evident you were being subjected to a severe setdown at her hands."

"If I suspected someone of stealing from me, I should be angry, too. Lady Wolcot does not know where I reside, but it will not be long before she does. I fear for Sir Arthur and Lady Betteridge, for she is certain to take them in dislike."

He smiled again. "You must not on any account trouble your head on that score, ma'am. My sister and brother-in-law are quite able to hold their own with the likes of Lady Wolcot, and if they had any fears to the contrary, I am persuaded they would not have invited you to stay."

"And you, my lord. You have a vested interest. . . ."

"I shall not deny it," he responded, and her heart sank. "That is why I am becoming a little impatient to see this matter resolved, for all our sakes."

She looked at him in dismay, and he went to sit on the edge of a large library table. He considered her carefully for a moment or two before flicking open the lid of his gold snuffbox and taking a leisurely pinch.

"It might well be politic," he said at last, "to stir up the coals a little now that Lady Wolcot has noted that you are still residing in London."

"Oh no!" she gasped.

"You are obliged to admit nothing has yet been resolved."

"What do you propose I should do?" she asked, curiosity getting the better of her fear.

"So far Lady Wolcot and whoever stole the snuffboxes are of the opinion you have no influence in this town. That is why you have been unable to refute her accusation with any credence."

"That is true. . . ."

"If it became known that you did, after all, have influential friends in London . . ."

As he spoke, Serafina began to wring her hands. "I cannot countenance such a thing, my lord. You and your family have been kind enough without becoming embroiled in this horrible affair any further."

"As you have quite rightly pointed out, Lady Wolcot is bound to discover where you are before much longer. Nothing remains hidden in this town forever, not even for a short time. There are those who know my brother-in-law has engaged an archivist—he has made no secret of the fact—and Lady Wolcot is not so woolly-headed not to come to a certain conclusion before too long."

He stood up when she remained silent, saying, "I understand your wish for anonymity all too well, for facing your accusers will not be easy or pleasant for you."

He came up to her again, and she found his closeness caused her even more discomposure. "I cannot conceive how such a course will help," she whispered.

"Hiding away has solved nothing," he pointed out. "And I have thought on this matter at length. No solution is possible if you continue in this manner. Hiding away can be construed as guilt just as much as running away to the country. I believe I have already made mention of that opinion."

Serafina was suddenly thoughtful. "What has prompted you to broach the subject again, my lord? Can it be you have some suspicions as to the real culprit?"

Her eyes were slightly narrowed as she watched him carefully. There was nothing to discern in his manner, and she did not wonder he was known to be such a renowned gamester, for he would never betray his card by gesture or expression.

"I confess to having a theory or two, that is all. Your brother tells me you suspect that Lady Wolcot herself might be the culprit."

"Oh, Jolyon had no right . . . !"

"He has your best interests at heart, my dear,

and I make no apologies for speaking to him. In any event he wished to please me; he requires sponsoring for several clubs."

Irritably she asked, "What do you suggest I do? Procure vouchers for Almack's?"

He smiled again. "I believe what we wish to achieve can be done without resorting to such extreme measures, although if vouchers to Almack's would serve the trick, I assure you they would be procured."

He took a few thoughtful steps away from her while she watched anxiously for him to announce what he proposed to do, for she did not doubt he had formulated some plan in his mind.

"The matter is bound to be brought to the forefront if, for instance . . ." he turned to gaze at her for a long moment, ". . . you and I announce our betrothal."

That this was his plan came as such a shocking surprise to her, she shied away from him. "My lord!" she gasped.

"The real thief would no longer have cause for complacency if he believed he had me to deal with, don't you agree?"

"Perchance you are correct on that score, my lord, but you cannot possibly expect me to countenance such a move."

"No?" he asked, raising his eyebrows slightly. "I think it is a splendid notion, especially in the event no one else has thought of a better one."

She laughed then, mirthlessly. "You are bamming me, aren't you?"

" 'Pon my honor, ma'am, I do not."

"No one would believe such a sham."

"I do not agree. I have been known to challenge the odds on more than one occasion before."

Again Serafina laughed. "Oh, I do not doubt it for one moment." Then she asked, "What about Imogen?"

"She can be told in due course. I daresay she would want you to be vindicated."

"But if she believes you are to marry *me* . . ."

"It is of no account, for this matter will be resolved very soon, and she will know the truth."

"Oh, you are very certain of yourself, my lord."

"Nothing else will serve," he answered with maddening complacency.

"No, 'tis impossible," she decided. "Your name, when it is linked with mine in the manner you propose, will be besmirched, and I cannot countenance that."

"It is kind of you to think it, ma'am, but I cannot agree. My grandfather married an actress, and a great aunt ran off with a groom. They did not give a straw about tattle and neither do I. The important point is that once it is known you are betrothed to me, Lady Wolcot will not dare slander you."

"Of course not, but she will drop a little poison here a little there, you may be certain."

"Do you really believe I give a fig for anything Lady Wolcot chooses to do or say?"

She turned to face him again. "I am of the opinion you regard this as something of a lark, my lord."

His face was devoid of expression, his dark, brooding gaze fathomless. "Think what you choose,

Miss D'Arblay. Are you prepared to wager your good name against a favorable outcome to this matter?" When she made no reply, he said mockingly, "I believed you to be a woman of great spirit."

He moved closer, putting his hands on her arms and drawing her toward him. As if mesmerized, Serafina could not resist.

"Would it be too difficult for you to pretend to love me, Serafina?" he asked in a soft, persuasive voice.

She looked up into his face, so close to hers. "Any woman would be proud to love you," she whispered.

Her lips were ready when his gently met hers. He could not mistake her response, and he was smiling as he drew away from her a few moments later.

"There now, you underestimate your own ability, my dear. You pretend admirably well." As he moved away from her at last, he said, in a more businesslike manner, "Allow me to think on this further for a day or two. I will inform my sister of what we propose to do, but you must not on any account discuss it with anyone else. Good day, Miss D'Arblay."

As the door closed behind him, Serafina sank down into a chair and covered her face with her hands, which she discovered were shaking. She had been so unprepared for the feelings his kiss had stirred up inside her. The kiss had been so brief and gentle, but there was also a hint of passion there, and it was to that she had responded so wholeheartedly, and to her utter humiliation there was no doubt he was aware of it, too.

The scheme he proposed was madness, she decided. The odds against success enormous. Naturally she recognized that was exactly why he was in favor of it. He was wagering his future with Imogen against the chance of her vindication. To a consummate gamester like Robert Trenton such odds would be most attractive she did not doubt.

As far as Serafina was concerned, her dire situation was no longer her prime consideration; she just wished that the imaginary betrothal could have been a real one.

For the remainder of the day Serafina threw herself into her work with even more zealousness than was usual, and she made considerable progress.

Fortunately Sir Arthur and Lady Betteridge were not at home for dinner that evening, so she was not obliged to face them, for she would not have known how to converse with them.

Despite her work-induced weariness, Serafina still found sleep elusive that night. Visions of Lord Trenton's face hovering close to hers haunted the night. Whenever she closed her eyes, she could still see his mocking face and feel the gentle brush of his lips on hers.

By morning she wished desperately she had never aquiesced to his plan, knowing at the same time she had never tacitly given her agreement to the scheme at all. Guiltily she also knew she should have firmly declined this particular offer for help, which she was convinced had no real chance of success. Then there was a secret part of her that would enjoy the pretense of being his future wife for the short time it would last.

When Serafina came down the following morning, a little later than usual for her, to her relief she found only Sir Arthur in the breakfast room. Much as she normally enjoyed Lady Betteridge's company, she really didn't know how she was going to be able to discuss Lord Trenton's proposal with her. Serafina found she had little appetite, but over a cup of coffee she discussed her progress with Sir Arthur, something of which she was much more sure.

"How did you contrive to achieve so much yesterday?" he asked in amazement.

"I applied myself to the task in hand," she explained.

"Mayhap it was my being out all day. I shall endeavor to absent myself as much as possible in the future."

Serafina could not help but laugh. "Oh, I entreat you not to do so, sir. Not on my account."

"In all truth I was quite prepared to see you slow your progress now that your brother is come to town."

"You mustn't think so, sir. My brother, in any event, will busy himself enjoying the pleasures of London."

Sir Arthur laughed. "So he should, even if it was not his very first visit."

He retreated behind the pages of the *Morning Post* when his ebullient wife appeared. "I declare you both put me to the blush being abroad so early."

"You evidently returned home very late last night, my lady," Serafina suggested.

She was glad to exchange pleasantries with Lady Betteridge and then excuse herself. However, as she did so, her ladyship said, "Miss D'Arblay, I am bound to say you look a trifle peaked this morning."

Serafina smiled faintly, knowing it was undoubtedly so. "I am quite robust, I thank you, my lady. You must not concern yourself for me."

"But I do! You have dark shadows beneath your eyes. I believe you are working too hard."

On hearing this remark, her husband looked around the newspaper. "Do not, on any account, accuse me of driving Miss D'Arblay like a slave, my dear."

"I assure you I am enjoying my work, my lady."

"That is all very well, my dear, and I do not for one moment doubt it, but you do not seem to take the air at all. You just closet yourself away in the library all day which cannot be good for you. Mayhap I can persuade you to cry off for a short while today."

"I really don't . . ."

"Why don't you accompany me to Swan and Edgar this morning? It isn't far, and we can walk. It will do you good to take the air. My niece, Dottie Betteridge, is getting married in the near future, and I wish to purchase a few gewgaws for her trousseau. Your advice will be invaluable."

"It is very kind of you to think of me, my lady, and I don't wish to be disobliging, but I really cannot. . . ."

"Tush! My husband will not mind if you take a brief break from your duties, will you, Arthur dear? Do tell Miss D'Arblay she must take the air with me this morning."

Sir Arthur put down the paper, and shaking his head said, "I certainly do not mind. Go along, child. Her ladyship is quite correct, you do need a respite. It will do you good, and therefore, I also insist upon it."

"Go along and fetch your bonnet and pelisse," Lady Betteridge told her, eyeing her indulgently. "We shall enjoy a coze during our outing, I fancy. We have had so few opportunities up until now."

It was immediately evident to Serafina that the subject Lady Betteridge wished to discuss was that of Lord Trenton's proposal, and it was with a heavy heart she returned to the hall a short while later to join her. Sure enough, as they set out from Betteridge House along Piccadilly, followed by a footman who would carry home their purchases, Lady Betteridge wasted no more time in broaching the subject Serafina dreaded.

"I had words with my brother yesterday evening, Miss D'Arblay, and you can well envisage the subject of our conversation. I confess to being quite overcome by his notion, and I am bound to confess I do not like this crackbrained scheme of his."

"I am in total agreement with you on that score, my lady."

The woman looked surprised. "Then why did you agree? Oh, do not trouble your head to reply to that, my dear," she went on quickly, waving her gloved hand in the air. "I have been acquainted with my brother for long enough to appreciate he would have scarce heeded you once his mind was made up."

"Mayhap you will be able to persuade him of the folly of this course."

"I very much doubt it, my dear."

"Do you believe we have any chance of success?" Serafina asked her hesitantly.

Lady Betteridge drew in a sharp breath. "I do not exactly know what my brother has in mind, the truth to tell, but he always goes into everything with good cards, and I do trust his judgment implicitly in all matters. However, I am afraid he is rather fond of taking risks and always enjoys sailing close to the wind." At almost every step they took, they were accosted by peddlars selling all manner of wares. So engrossed was Serafina in their conversation, she scarcely noticed them as the footman shooed them away. "Just as long as we don't all go home by Weeping Cross," her ladyship added wryly.

Serafina did not feel in any way reassured, but merely replied, "I would not want his lordship to jeopardize his future."

Lady Betteridge glanced at her strangely. "He is far too astute to do such a thing. It really is too late to provide you with suitable attire for this . . . little masquerade, but my daughter, who you may be aware is married and ruralizing just now, left behind her various garments that will suit you admirably."

"Will that really be necessary?"

"My dear, you are, you know, extraordinarily

fetching, and in modish attire you would be quite breathtaking."

Serafina's cheeks grew pink. "You are too kind, my lady."

"I assure you I am not bamming you, but of far more import than your pride, is appearing a suitable bride for my brother."

"No one can possibly believe that."

"You do yourself great injustices, Miss D'Arblay. I assure you *everyone* will believe it. The sham begins this afternoon."

Serafina looked startled. "I had no notion it would be so soon."

"There is no possible advantage to waiting any longer. In any event, there is a regatta on the Thames this afternoon. Robert believes it an ideal opportunity to have you by his side in public. Everyone will be on or at the river today. You will be delighted to learn that Mr. D'Arblay is escorting Miss Geddes."

"Oh, Imogen . . ." Serafina gasped.

"I am bound to confess I am of the opinion your brother is an exceedingly charming young man."

Again Serafina's cheeks grew pink. "So is yours, my lady," she replied, and Lady Betteridge laughed.

"Yes, you are quite correct, Miss D'Arblay, and while we are upon the subject, you will be interested to know that when I conversed with Miss Geddes yesterday, she was complaining bitterly that your brother was paying too much attention to various young ladies."

Serafina looked agreeably surprised before saying, "The minx. I daresay it is quite in order for her to flirt, but not for poor Jolyon. Thank you, my lady, for that is very satisfying news. Had Imogen not cared about my brother's attention to others, that would have given me cause for concern."

Messrs. Swan and Edgar's new emporium at the corner of Piccadilly was a haven for shoppers. Distracted from her discomforting thoughts, Serafina was happy to help choose various items Lady Betteridge wished to purchase for her niece. The shop was rather crowded with well-dressed people, and on numerous occasions Lady Betteridge paused to exchange a word with an acquaintance, and to Serafina's relief she was introduced merely as Miss D'Arblay "our houseguest."

Most people merely cast her curious looks, no doubt wondering just who she could be to warrant the condescension of Lady Betteridge. However, others were much more obvious in their interests, and to her chagrin Serafina was convinced they had heard her name on the lips of Lady Wolcot.

Suddenly as she and Lady Betteridge made their way out of the emporium, her ladyship let out an unexpected peal of laughter.

"Miss D'Arblay, I beg you to forgive me. I was only just contemplating the furor that will ensue when it becomes known you have become betrothed to my brother."

Serafina looked away in distress. "Have you thought about the tattle that is bound to ensue when he cries off after our betrothal has served its purpose—or not?"

All at once her ladyship became serious. "I fully

appreciate your concern, but you must not trouble your head on that score. You will be extricated from this with no embarrassment attached to you."

"I daresay I shall be glad enough to be extricated from the taint of being a thief, if that is at all possible, which I am bound to admit, I doubt," she replied.

She did not go on to say that no one would be in the least surprised that Lord Trenton had cried off his marriage. She had no standing in society, and no one expected someone as elevated as Viscount Trenton to marry a penniless nobody. The *ton* would heave a collective sigh of relief that on this occasion their elusive ranks would not be breached by an aspiring mushroom.

Lady Betteridge was casting Serafina a concerned look when both ladies became aware that a carriage had drawn up at the curb, and Lady Wolcot was being handed down by her footman.

"This could not be more opportune," Lady Betteridge confided in a whisper.

Serafina's first instinct was to hurry away, but she quickly acknowledged the time for doing so was now at an end. With Lord Trenton and Lady Betteridge behind her, she could afford to be more forthcoming and no longer hide away from the unpleasantness of the situation.

The moment she set eyes upon Serafina, the countess looked even more shocked than she had when she had seen her at Vauxhall Gardens, for it was now evident who exactly were the friends harboring her. The disbelief on Lady Wolcot's florid face was almost comical to see had Serafina not felt so nervous.

When Lady Betteridge asked, "Lady Wolcot, have you come to see the excellent goods on sale here?" the countess's face contorted into an angry grimace, and she strode toward them with a purposeful air.

"Lady Betteridge, I must protest now it is obvious to me who is harboring this felon. I confess to be disappointed to discover you have taken up the very creature who has caused me such grief."

Lady Betteridge held up her gloved hand, while Serafina studied with interest the ground beneath her feet. "My lady, before you continue this set-down, I feel I must tell you that the reason I was obliged to take Miss D'Arblay into my establishment was on the behest of my brother."

Lady Wolcot looked even more taken aback. "I cannot believe his lordship to be so imprudent, even at the behest of my cork-brained goddaughter."

Lady Betteridge continued to smile apologetically. "You must not blame Miss Geddes in this matter, for I am quite persuaded she knows nothing of it. However, you must surely know how foolish gentlemen are likely to behave when they have fixed their interest. . . ."

The countess's eyes started out of their sockets. "Fixed his interest? Do you mean . . . ?" A faint smile came to her lips. "The minx has yet to tell me, so I do beg your forgiveness, my lady, if . . ."

Lady Betteridge laughed lightly. "Oh no, my dear, you mistake my meaning entirely."

The smile quickly faded from the countess's lips. "I do? Then pray what is your meaning?"

"I am indeed a chucklehead not to make myself more plain. My brother is about to announce his betrothal to . . . Miss D'Arblay."

*"What?"* Serafina was forced to contain her own chuckles, which were welling up inside her. "You cannot mean to imply that this bit of muslin and Lord Trenton . . ."

Lady Betteridge nodded emphatically. When Serafina glanced at her sideways, she could see she was enjoying herself hugely. For Serafina's part she considered the countess's discomfiture small revenge for the anguish she had caused her.

"Indeed I do," Lady Betteridge went on. "In fact, my lady, you are one of the first to know of this matter. Lord Trenton and Miss D'Arblay will soon announce their coming marriage officially, but as yet few know of it."

For a moment Serafina thought once again that Lady Wolcot might succumb to a seizure. Her bosom heaved beneath her fur-lined pelisse, her face became suffused with color, and her eyes bulged unnaturally.

"Surely you are roasting me," she gasped at last. "He had almost certainly fixed his interest with my goddaughter."

All at once Lady Betteridge looked very serious. "I assure you, I am not roasting you, my lady."

Suddenly Lady Wolcot's eyes narrowed as she transferred her attention to the silent Serafina. "You doxy!" she accused, and Lady Betteridge broke in quickly.

"Oh my dear Lady Wolcot, recall you are addressing the future Lady Trenton."

The countess's lips snapped shut. "You must forgive me . . . the shock of it. My poor goddaughter . . . her distress when she comes to hear of it. She is foremost in my thoughts just now."

"We fully understand your shock," Lady Betteridge sympathized. "When you return home, you will discover an invitation awaiting you. It is to an informal party to celebrate their coming nuptials. Naturally, Miss D'Arblay was anxious for Miss Geddes to attend and to indicate her utter goodness, she insisted—yes, insisted, Lady Wolcot—that you be invited, also. She is quite exceptional, don't you agree?"

"Really!" the countess gasped, placing one hand to her breast and staggering slightly backward.

Lady Betteridge continued to smile in a conciliatory manner, and Serafina found her own lips twitching. "It is evident to my brother and myself that some idiotic error was made at your establishment soon after Miss D'Arblay arrived in London. None of us, and in particular Miss D'Arblay, wishes to continue being at daggers drawn with you. Is that not so, Miss D'Arblay?"

"Oh, indeed," she agreed, enjoying the countess's obvious discomfort.

"Nor would Lord Trenton. We are all quite persuaded an error was made and accusations bandied about, which I am certain you have come to know were unnecessary. Naturally, his lordship would not wish his betrothed to suffer any further distress in this matter, so do come along and show that you, too, are ready to affect a reconciliation. Miss D'Arblay, I do not doubt, would become Lady Trenton with a much happier heart if you could see your way to do so."

"Really!" the countess gasped again.

Lady Betteridge subjected her to the most guileless of smiles. "Until then, my lady."

Serafina bobbed a quick curtsy, but it was not until they had walked away a few paces that both allowed themselves to laugh out loud at last. Serafina glanced back to see that Lady Wolcot was now scolding her footman on some matter.

Then she returned her attention to Lady Betteridge, who said, "Well, my dear, I am very much afraid that there is no going back now."

Serafina shivered slightly, although she was not certain whether it was through fear or excitement.

# TWELVE

Serafina was still in this contradictory mood when Lord Trenton arrived in his curricle to convey her to the regatta. All arrangements had been made without prior consultation with her, which in any event she would not have expected. She just wished it had not been arranged for her to be the sole occupant in the viscount's curricle.

Eyeing him covertly, she thought he looked extremely handsome, wearing a buff-colored riding coat, and as always his neck cloth was tied immaculately in the style known as *tron d'amour*. His Hessian boots bore a high shine, and there was not one wrinkle to be seen in his skintight buckskin pantaloons.

"I was a little afraid that you might have cried off by now," he told her, as she tied her bonnet strings into a great bow at her cheek.

Serafina suspected he was challenging her in some manner and admitted as he handed her onto the box, "I have been tempted to do so, my lord, for most of the past four and twenty hours."

"I knew you had more pluck than to do so."

"Mayhap I just have windmills in my head," she retorted, which just made him laugh.

The curricle, she noted, was being drawn by the same team she had admired on their first encounter.

"I welcome this opportunity to drive you, Serafina," he told her. "To prove to you at last my driving is not always reckless."

Her cheeks colored at his reminding her of that episode, which she fervently wished forgotten.

When he climbed up beside her and took up the ribbons, she told him, "I have never sailed on a river before, so it is quite a novelty to me."

"Whereas a betrothal you take entirely in your stride."

Serafina ignored his teasing and went on, staring straight ahead of her, "Indeed, I have only once been in a boat, and that was a small rowboat on a lake."

"It is something of a novelty for me, too, to escort a lady who is not already bored with every diversion."

"You may just call me a greenhorn," she retorted.

The viscount smiled as they set off. "I fear you are being peevish only because you are fearful of what will happen, but you need have no cause for concern."

"I am obliged to hear that you think not."

Again he smiled. "I trust you are not the type of female who indulges in *mal de mer* the moment she claps eyes upon the water."

"That all depends upon the type of vessel we are

to be sailing in. I am bound to tell you that if we are to navigate the length of the Thames in a small rowboat, you might well have cause for concern."

"And if I tell you we will be sailing in my yacht?"

She looked at him in amazement then. "Indeed?" Then she looked away again. "I daresay that makes me feel very much better."

"It should. Scores of people would give a good deal for an invitation to board my yacht. You, my dear Serafina, are about to become the most envied female in London."

She glanced at him again, her eyes narrowed this time. "Your boastfulness is only exceeded by your arrogance, my lord. It is as well I am not well-known in your circles, for anyone who is in the least acquainted with me would be certain I would not agree to marry a man so high in the instep."

"I must consider myself suitably chastened, ma'am," he replied, and when she cast him a surreptitious look, she suspected he was laughing at her.

However, she did regret her waspishness and said in a more compliant manner, "I do beg your pardon, my lord. My nerves are considerably overset, as you might guess."

"If you believe I only enjoy conversing with toad-eaters you could not be more mistaken."

She smiled then, relaxing somewhat. "I daresay you encounter many who only seek to grease your boots."

"It is good for my esteem," he answered with a laugh, "and, moreover, you will come to agree with me after you have been thought to be my bride-to-be for a little while. You will be engulfed by toadies."

Serafina did not want to discuss the matter of her false betrothal and said quickly, "Tell me about your yacht. Is it a coincidence it is on the river just now?"

"No. I keep it moored here while I'm in town in the event any member of the family should wish to use her. One day soon, when this wretched war is finally over, I intend to sail to France, but enough of that," he decided, glancing at her at the same time as expertly handling the team through the traffic.

Serafina could not help but admire his skill; however, she had no intention of telling him of her opinion of his driving.

They were not the only people who wished to attend the regatta. It appeared that most of London's population were on their way there, too.

"Do you feel confident about what we are doing?" he asked.

She laughed without mirth. "I wish I knew exactly what you had in mind, my lord."

"It is best you do not, Miss D'Arblay . . . Serafina," he replied, and she looked away from him in great confusion.

"Lady Betteridge says you always go in with good cards."

He laughed again. "She is quite correct, you may be sure. When we were children, I invariably involved her in wild larks, but she will tell you I always got her out of them with no real difficulty."

"Then I must content myself with that knowledge."

"This ruse will effect a great revenge upon Lady Wolcot for her cruel behavior toward you. You may derive satisfaction from that. You might even consider it worthwhile allying yourself to me to achieve it."

The approach to the river was a seething mass of people who had no access to a sailing vessel but were nonetheless determined to enjoy the day. They waved flags and availed themselves of prodigious amounts of heavy-wet, which was available at booths. Somewhere close by a band was playing, adding to the festive atmosphere.

Serafina looked amazed at so much activity, as the viscount edged his team along. "Does this happen often?" she asked.

"Usually it is in aid of someone's birthday. I believe today it is the Princess Charlotte's."

When they finally arrived at Lord Trenton's yacht, Serafina was once again amazed, this time at the size of the vessel. It appeared very large to her and was manned by a full crew. After handing the care of his curricle and team to his tiger, Lord Trenton escorted Serafina aboard *Elfrida*, and then he went to consult with the captain, no doubt to go over plans for the rest of the afternoon.

For the moment Serafina was utterly diverted from her problems by the gay sight of a river with its carpet of boats and barges of all sizes, trimmed with flags and filled with people. Over the noise of the band playing on the river's edge came the peal of bells from St. Margaret's Church. Westminster

Bridge, a short distance away from the moored yacht, was choked with people, and either side of it was congested by gaming tables that she could see were being well patronized.

After a few minutes the viscount joined her on the deck. "My apologies for leaving you, Serafina, but I wanted to ensure that everything is as it should be for my guests. The picnic hamper has arrived from Gunter's, so we shall not go hungry!"

"I seriously doubt that I shall be able to eat a morsel," she declared, shivering slightly.

"Have I not already told you? You must have no fear today, Serafina. Only friends will be present this afternoon. Lady Wolcot has not been invited. There was not time."

"We encountered her this morning."

"Did you indeed?" he asked, his eyes narrowing with interest. "I'll warrant that was a most intriguing encounter."

"Lady Betteridge informed her of our . . . forthcoming betrothal."

He laughed. "I'll wager that caused her to get into a bobble."

Serafina could not help but laugh at the recollection. "You are quite correct on that score, my lord. She appeared very much affected by the news, and I cannot help but feel we were very cruel."

He gazed at her oddly then. "How remarkably forgiving you are. No one could have been more cruel than Lady Wolcot in her Turkish treatment of you, and yet I suspect you pity her."

"You have never doubted my innocence, and I cannot help but wonder why."

He looked somewhat amused. "My dear Serafina, it is patently obvious to anyone other than a hopeless imbecile that anyone so open in her manner could not possibly be underhanded enough to steal her hostess's property."

Their eyes met, and the glance that passed between them seemed to last an unconscionably long time and caused her heart to flutter unevenly, until the unmistakable voice of Lady Betteridge broke the spell.

"What a struggle it was for us to get here!" she gasped as she came on board. "I declare I have seen nothing like it in my life before. We were obliged in the end to walk at least a hundred yards. It was no use attempting to ride any farther."

Lord Trenton went to greet them warmly, and Lady Betteridge conveyed a worried look across to Serafina. She had arrived in the company of her niece, Dottie Betteridge and her husband-to-be, Lieutenant Buckler of the Life Guards. It came as no surprise to Serafina that Sir Arthur had taken the opportunity of remaining at home, where he could have the library to himself for a change.

"My dear Miss D'Arblay, I was never more surprised—nay shocked—than when Aunt Mira told me your astonishing and delightful news," Dottie Betteridge announced when she caught sight of Serafina.

The declaration caused Serafina to blush with confusion, and Lieutenant Buckler said to Lord Trenton, "Allow me to be the first to wish you happy, my lord."

Just then Serafina felt wretched as well as embarrassed. She had become fully prepared to act the hummer to Lady Wolcot and her cronies, but to Lord Trenton's friends and family it was going to be a little more difficult to sustain the act, for they had always been so kind to her.

"All this talk of weddings is sublime," Dottie confided delightedly. "And I am bound to confess myself delighted that his lordship did not, after all, choose some bread-and-butter miss."

Noting her discomposure, Lord Trenton hurried to her side. "My bride-to-be as you may have noted, Dottie, is the most modest and unassuming lady. It is not difficult to put her to the blush."

Dottie Betteridge eyed him cheekily from beneath the brim of her bonnet. "Miss D'Arblay is a refreshing change to the kind of females in whose company you are usually to be found."

Not at all put out the viscount retorted, "Dottie, my dear child, I shall accept that declaration as a compliment."

"It was meant to be, I assure you. We could not be more delighted that you are about to be riveted. Just wait until I tell Mama and Papa. They believe you to be an incurable rakehell with no hope of redemption!"

Again he laughed. "Am I meant to take that as a compliment, too, you abominable wretch?"

"Most gentlemen would do so," she retorted.

Just then Serafina gasped when she caught sight of Imogen, escorted by Jolyon, coming aboard the yacht. She, too, looked as bewildered as Serafina had been by all the crowds and noise. Jolyon waved happily to his sister, but immediately went to address Lieutenant Buckler on some score, although Imogen came running up to Serafina, her cheeks flushed and her eyes bright.

"Oh, you sly creature!" The girl grasped her friend's hands and squeezed them tightly in hers. "I declare myself all a mort! I could not believe my ears when Lady Wolcot returned home in such a pelter this morning. I was of the firm opinion she had taken leave of her senses when she announced that you and Lord Trenton were betrothed. It is true though, is it not? Do say that it is!"

Serafina uneasily and unwillingly confirmed the fact.

"It is entirely right that you will be married before me. After all, you are somewhat older."

Serafina laughed mirthlessly. "We had all believed me on the shelf, Imogen."

"How wicked of you not to have so much as hinted at the possibility of a match with his lordship! I shall not easily forgive you, you may be certain. Well, at least we have solved the vexing question as to who was the creature Lord Trenton waltzed with in his sister's music room. All the drawing rooms are awash with tattle about it. I had no notion it was you, Serafina."

"Imogen . . ." Her friend began in an attempt to change the subject.

However, the young lady was not so easily silenced. "Poor Lady Wolcot, she was entirely overset. We were obliged to administer hartshorn the moment she arrived back, but in the end her maid burned feathers, and we were bound to consider the option of sending for her physician she was in such a taking. How I wish you had confided in me first though, just a tiny hint would have been sufficient. I have always confided in *you*."

"It happened so quickly," Serafina replied.

"Needless to say her ladyship would be furious if she knew I was here with you and Jolyon, but fortunately she has developed the most tormenting headache and has retired to her room with a dose of laudanum. Oh, I am a wicked creature to think so," Imogen chuckled, "but I, for one, could not be more delighted for you."

Serafina looked amazed. "Truly?"

"How can you doubt it? I always considered you too good to be obliged to earn your living in such a way."

"So you do not harbor any fondness for Lord Trenton . . . ?"

The young woman looked scathing. "Indeed not. That was all in Lady Wolcot's mind. In truth, dearest," she went on, lowering her voice, "since my arrival, I have not met one gentleman who matches up in any way to my dear Jolyon."

"Imogen . . ." Serafina began in a warning tone.

"Listen to me, dearest. Can you not see that the solution is now at hand? When you are Lady Trenton, you can take me up. In that event Mama and Papa can have no objection to Jolyon. You will be very important in the beau monde, and there is nothing to prevent you bringing me out!"

Serafina felt more wretched than ever. She was very much tempted to tell Imogen she never would be Lady Trenton, and there was no possible way in which she could help her, but she knew she must remain silent on the matter. The dilemma was, however, a painful one. Fortunately Jolyon approached her then, and Imogen, casting him a shy look, went to the rail to join Dottie Betteridge, who was watching the activity on the river and pointing out interesting sights.

"Oh, Sal, how happy I am for you. This is the most splendid news I have ever heard. You have always deserved the very best, and now you are about to have everything I would wish for you. Lord Trenton is a fine fellow, none better in my opinion. Not only have you made a most splendid match, you have removed one of my closest rivals for Imogen's hand."

"Joly, you really are being a trifle premature," she reasoned.

"I know it, but the possibilities are exciting for me as well as you, dearest. When you are married to someone so plump in the pocket, there will be no problem about buying my commission, and as my sister will be Lady Trenton, who could possibly object to my paying court to Imogen?"

"Your sister would still be regarded as a mushroom, I fear," she pointed out.

"Humbug!" he responded. "I cannot conceive why you are not crying roast meat. Any other female would be strutting like a crow in the gutter on being so elevated by marriage."

"I cannot be in high gig until the official announcement has gone into the *Morning Post*," she told him in desperation. "Where did you obtain the funds to buy yet another new coat?"

"From my allowance. I have had precious little to spend the blunt on until now. Do you not think I am in prime style?"

"Oh indeed. A regular out and outer, I don't doubt."

He touched his neck cloth. "I saw Beau Brummell at White's last night, and his neck cloth was folded exactly in this manner. He was sitting in the bow window as usual with 'Poodle' Byng and Lord Alvanley."

"Where did you obtain the gig in which you drove Imogen down here this afternoon? Your allowance cannot possibly cover the cost of that."

"Do you know, Sal? You are turning into a shrew. I feel it incumbent upon me to warn Trenton of this trait in you. I cannot allow such a first-rater to become your tenant for life without at least a warning."

"Do as you please," Serafina replied, "but you still have not told me where you obtained the gig."

"The gig is hired from Mr. Tilbury and will be returned to him as soon as I have delivered Imogen back to Wolcot House."

The arrival just then of Sir Philip Chorton and the Earl of Granton enabled them to set sail at last, and Serafina was glad to join the others at the rail to discuss, hopefully, something other than her betrothal.

*Elfrida* slipped gently away from her moorings to the good-natured cheering of those on the bank. On the river, skiffs and barges full of young bucks, most of whom were rather the worse for drink, sped past the yacht as they made their way toward Greenwich.

Despite her inner turmoil, Serafina could not help but be stirred by the sights before her, even more so when the royal yacht was seen coming toward them. The flying of the Prince Regent's own standard on the mast indicated he was on board, but only Princess Charlotte could be seen on deck cheered by her subjects as the yacht sailed by.

"What a pity he remained below deck," Imogen lamented. "I have not yet set eyes upon Prinny, and I am in a fidge to do so."

"If he is at all sensible, he will remain below deck and view everything from there," Miss Betteridge observed. "He is not the most popular gentleman in London just now and can only attract booing whenever he goes abroad."

"I have noted that no one can speak well of His Royal Highness," Imogen admitted, "which is a most dreadful thing when it concerns one's future king."

"It is said that he has become a trifle afraid of assassination attempts since Mr. Percival was murdered earlier this year," Dottie informed her.

"Poor Prinny," Imogen murmured, and then turning to Serafina, confided, "I cannot recall enjoying myself so much since you left Wolcot House."

"Mayhap that is due in some measure to Jolyon's presence," Serafina ventured.

The girl's cheeks grew pink. "I cannot gainsay that statement, dearest. My only fear is that he may have fixed his interest elsewhere, for he has displayed inordinate interest in a number of females who, I may say, did not make a match last Season."

"Jolyon will only fix his interest with another if he decides there is no longer any hope of making a match with you. You surely cannot expect someone of Jolyon's looks and address to wear the willow forever."

While Imogen looked thoughtful Serafina went on, her manner concerned, "I do hope Lady Wolcot will not give you a severe setdown when you arrive back. I feel certain she would not wish you to be here with Jolyon and me."

"She surely cannot object to my being on Lord Trenton's yacht, under the watchful eye of Lady Betteridge."

"Even if Lord Trenton is betrothed to me?"

Imogen chuckled unexpectedly. "I am persuaded she took so much laudanum, she will remain in her room until the morrow and never know or even care where I have been. Is this not the most splendid yacht you have ever seen, Serafina?"

"It is the only one I have ever seen, apart from Prinny's," Serafina answered with a laugh, "and if you press me to say so, I am bound to declare His Royal Highness's vessel did not look anything as grand as this one!"

"Wait until you go below deck," Dottie volunteered. "It is most luxurious."

"I look forward to inspecting it after our picnic," Imogen told her. "I am already quite ravenous. The shock of your news must have given me an appetite!"

"Lord Trenton often entertains on board, and not only large parties like this one," Dottie added, looking mischievous.

She immediately shot an apologetic look toward Serafina, who said quickly, "It would be exceedingly crackbrained of me to believe I am the only female Lord Trenton has ever known."

Dottie laughed uncomfortably. "He has taken an unconscionable time to make his choice. I do feel very strongly you will be the last."

Serafina struggled to conceal her discomfort by venturing, "I daresay Elfrida was an exceptional woman in his life if he named his yacht after her. Did you know her, Miss Betteridge?"

"It is scarcely likely, Miss D'Arblay, for I daresay she was or still is some fashionable cyprian. There have been several to find favor in his eyes, I am told, but the name is certainly not familiar to me."

Even though what Miss Betteridge had to tell her was no surprise, Serafina nevertheless felt even more wretched, but she had no chance to recover before Lieutenant Buckler came to tell them the picnic was ready.

The crew had set out the contents of the basket, which brought forth gasps of admiration from the guests. An abundance of chicken and wafer-thin ham was set out for them, together with all manner of game pies and fish mousses. The delicate pastries, supplied by Gunter's, could not be faulted, even by Serafina, who felt that eating even a morsel would choke her.

"Come now," Lord Trenton urged, handing her a

piece of chicken and a slice of bread and butter, "you must eat a little more. You should be in such great spout you would eat *everything* put before you."

"I cannot eat and pretend at one and the same time," she complained, which made him smile.

"You are doing splendidly. I know it must be difficult for you."

"Evidently it is easy for you."

"Amazingly so," he replied, as he carefully wiped his fingers on a linen napkin embroidered with the yacht's name.

"I had not counted on everyone being so delighted for us."

"Nor I, but it is heartwarming, is it not?"

Serafina cast him a furious look. "I am not accustomed to being a hummer, my lord."

He glanced around at his guests before whispering, "Call me Robert, lest anyone should find your formality suspicious."

Serafina gasped with annoyance. "You do not, I fear, take this seriously."

He gave her a considering look that made her feel quite peculiar before he replied, "I do, be certain that I do."

When the crew members came to clear away the remains of their meal, she took the opportunity of wandering back to the rail, her wineglass still in her hand.

As she passed, Lady Betteridge whispered, "This is going far better than I supposed, my dear."

"I find it a difficult pretense to maintain, my lady."

"I warned my brother he was asking the impossible of you, but he is headstrong and stubborn. Naught is like to change him now."

"I cannot help but fear we are getting ourselves into a deep hole from which we might not be able to climb out."

"If so it will be the first time Robert has not been able to do so, I assure you."

When Dottie attracted her aunt's attention, Lady Betteridge reluctantly went to join her. Serafina noticed Imogen and Jolyon removing themselves to the far side of the deck. Just then she envied their devotion, although she knew, sadly, that they were no more likely to enjoy a happy ending than she.

Lord Trenton found her staring down into the water a few minutes later. "I beg your pardon most heartily, if you believe me making too light of all this."

"It is not that which troubles me," she confessed, looking up at him. "Imogen and Jolyon both look to me now to help them when I become Lady Trenton. I dare not imagine their dismay when it becomes known I cannot."

"Serafina, I am beginning to be out of patience with you," he told her, not unkindly. "For once and once only you must think of yourself. This is of the greatest import to *you*. Your future well-being depends upon your being able to prove your innocence. The worst that can happen to that young couple is their hearts will be a little bruised, and that is something that has caused no lasting harm to any of us."

She smiled faintly. "You have a very persuasive tongue, my lord."

"So I have often been told. I have also instructed you to call me Robert. That cannot be so difficult."

"I will try," she promised, but displayed little enthusiasm.

"You do not look in the least like a female who is newly betrothed."

"Mayhap that is because I am not."

"You are exceedingly disobliging, my girl. In any event you could not look more out of countenance than if Lady Wolcot had consigned you to Newgate. Perchance in that event you would have been as gay as a goose in a gutter."

Serafina suppressed a chuckle, as he added, "Do try to appear less blue-deviled, my dear." He cast a smile toward Dottie and Lieutenant Buckler as they strolled past along the deck. "Remember you have just made a great match. Females of every age will be looking at you with a rage of envy."

"You are so conceited," she chided, unable to take offense, owing to the lightness of his manner.

"It is not my fault if ninnyhammers insist upon making much of me."

"You're outrageous!" she accused.

"You are not the first to make that accusation either. Now remember, Serafina, you must contrive to look delighted with your good fortune and not act the surly-boots."

She could no longer suppress her laughter, which was no doubt his intention all along. "You must find me a trifle provoking at times, my . . . Robert."

She flushed slightly as he answered, leaning against the rail, the slight river breeze ruffling his dark curls, "Provoking indeed, but females invariably are, I find."

Serafina gasped and then chided, "Even Elfrida?" When he looked at her in some surprise, she added, "The original Elfrida I mean. You must have cared for her very much to name your yacht in her honor."

When he looked at her again, his eyes were filled with amusement. "Ah yes, Elfrida. You are not mistaken, for I loved her desperately as only a callow youth is able."

"Was she very beautiful?" Serafina asked in a small voice, wishing she had not broached the subject after all.

"Oh, indeed she was," he replied, his mind far away. "You can scarce conceive of her beauty, Serafina." He glanced at her again. "She was without doubt, the most beautiful creature I can ever recall. Her coloring was very dark, not at all different from yours. Everyone admired that mane of dark hair and the most melting brown eyes."

"Do you still see her?" she asked, not really wanting to know, but unable to stop herself asking.

"Alas no. She died some time ago, but I still miss her. She was, Serafina, the best horse I have ever owned."

For a moment or two she stared at him uncomprehendingly and then began to laugh. Not only was the day the best Imogen had experienced since arriving in London, but all at once Serafina began to experience a similar feeling.

# THIRTEEN

"I shall be more than a little relieved when all this tarradiddle is over," Sir Arthur commented one day when he came into the library. "Can't see the sense in it myself."

"Nor I, if the truth be told, sir," Serafina replied, looking somewhat troubled, "and I most heartily beg your pardon for the interruption in my work. I would be more than happy for you to suspend my salary until it is over."

"Wouldn't consider it. My library and family documents have been in such a shambles for so long, I daresay they can wait a little longer before being put to rights. Besides, you have made more than a good start on them already, and if Trenton believes this humgudgeon is necessary, I am inclined to believe him."

Serafina looked at him in surprise. "You are?"

"Oh yes," Sir Arthur answered earnestly. "He was a trifle rackety in his youth, but he is basically sound, although I cannot imagine what he is trying to do. When he first broached the subject, I thought I'd given him too much port! Now, did you have any ideas on what we should do with those diaries of my grandmother, Miss D'Arblay?"

"Oh yes, I thought . . ."

A knock on the door heralded the arrival of a footman, carrying a silver tray. "There is a caller for Miss D'Arblay, Sir Arthur. A Mrs. Wallace Wyndham declares herself anxious to have words with Miss D'Arblay."

As Sir Arthur clucked his tongue with impatience Serafina replied, "I am afraid I cannot see anyone just now. I am much too busy."

"No, no," Sir Arthur contradicted. "You run along and see Mrs. Wyndham. As the future Lady Trenton, you are bound to be in great demand, and I must strive to remember that."

Serafina shot him a grateful look. "You may be quite certain, Sir Arthur, when all this is over, I will work twice as hard."

He laughed as she hurried from the room, saying, "I intend to remind you of that promise, Miss D'Arblay."

Caroline Wyndham had been shown into the small drawing room and was stripping off her York-kid gloves in a businesslike manner when Serafina came in, and she immediately jumped to her feet.

"Serafina! So it is true. You are here!"

"As you see, Caroline," Serafina replied, smiling in a rather strained manner.

"You have no notion how concerned I have been for you of late."

Serafina sat down on the sofa, facing her cousin's wife with a calmness she really did not feel. "There was no need, I assure you."

"So I observe! You look positively serene."

"Inside I am all aquiver," Serafina replied, in all honesty.

Caroline Wyndham looked coy. " 'Tis no wonder, you slyboots! You certainly know how to provide the tattle-baskets with their *on-dits*, my dear."

"It has not been deliberate, you may be certain."

"I know you well enough to believe that is so, but your name is now on everyone's lips." Caroline paused to eye Serafina carefully for a moment, and then she went on, "I confess I was as cross as two sticks when Wallace told me what had transpired between you the day you came to see him."

"You must not let it trouble you any longer."

"But I do! Had I been at home when you arrived that day, you may be certain you would not have been obliged to seek shelter elsewhere. I was quite mortified!"

"I do know it, dearest, and I wouldn't want you to get into a pucker over it now, or indeed be on the outs with Wallace."

Caroline smiled happily. "No indeed! After all, it has turned out so well in the end. How romantic it must be, although that does not excuse in the least my husband's Turkish treatment of you when you were in dire need of his help. If one cannot rely upon one's kith and kin in time of trouble, who can one possibly go to?"

"Sir Arthur and Lady Betteridge," Serafina supplied, and the woman smiled uncomfortably.

"It is quite amazing to think you were so close to us all the while. Naturally, I had no notion of that. When it was mentioned to me that Sir Arthur Betteridge had engaged someone to catalog his family documents I had no notion it was you. The day you came to our house, as soon as I had rung a peal over Wallace, I sat down to pen a note to you, which I sent immediately to you at Coverdale, naturally believing you to be there. When I received no reply, I'm afraid I assumed you were on the outs with me, too."

"By no means, Caroline, as you must now realize," Serafina replied.

It came as a profound shock to her to discover that Caroline was terrified of falling foul of the future Lady Trenton.

"I am so relieved to hear you say so. After all, dearest, we have always dealt so well together, and when you are Lady Trenton, you will preside over the most splendid establishment in Grosvenor Square." Serafina continued to stare down at her hands as Caroline began to gather her gloves and reticule together. "As soon as your betrothal is announced formally, I intend to throw a ball in your honor. It is the least I can do to make amends."

She got to her feet and kissed Serafina delightedly on the cheek. "You are causing such a sensation, my dear, and it will quite overshadow Miss Geddes's debut, which is a pity for the poor chit, but quite splendid for you. Now when anyone asks me if it is true Lord Trenton is to marry Miss D'Arblay, I can say it is so, and that we are very closely related. Now I know where you have hidden yourself, we shall not remain strangers. Good-bye for now, dearest."

Serafina had only a short time in which to catch

her breath before Lady Betteridge came hurrying into the house. "Was that Caroline Wyndham I saw leaving just now?"

Serafina, who had remained in the hall gathering her chaotic thoughts together, confirmed that it was. "Poor Caro had been plagued with those who wish to know about the betrothal. She is quite bewildered by all the to-do."

Lady Betteridge's eyes rolled upward as she removed her bonnet. "She is not alone, I assure you. I have been besieged wherever I have gone today. I have been approached by so many of those who are in a fidge to meet the bride-to-be, but they will all be obliged to wait until we have settled the matter of proving your innocence."

Serafina looked at her in bewilderment. "But, my lady, after that is done—if it is—I shall no longer be betrothed to his lordship."

The older lady put one hand to her head and laughed. "What a chucklehead I am to be sure! But there, if I have come to believe in it, everyone else must do so."

"I am surprised anyone believes it," Serafina told her. "We are scarce well matched."

"You would not be the first penniless girl to marry into the *ton*. Heavens, in my own family there were far odder alliances that caused a stir at the time, but were soon forgotten. Now, my dear," she went on briskly, "have you tried on those gowns I sent to your room this morning?"

"No, my lady. I have instead been attempting to continue with my work in the library."

"Faddle to that. Arthur is fully aware that most

needs be postponed for the time being. Go along and try the gowns on now, especially the lace evening gown. It is quite the most beautiful of them all, and I feel certain it will suit you very well indeed. I shall send Bridie along in the event any alterations need to be made."

When Serafina continued to hesitate, Lady Betteridge told her in some exasperation, "We really don't have any time to waste before our little soiree to introduce you formally as my brother's future wife."

"Am I correct in assuming, my lady, that Lady Wolcot has formally accepted your invitation?"

"Well, naturally she has. Lady Wolcot would not wish to miss the opportunity of being one of the first to wish my brother happy, or being able to tell her cronies she has met his bride-to-be."

"It is what she has already told them that troubles me."

"My dear, I shall not deride your very real feelings about her accusation, but I do believe you have exaggerated her influence to a great degree."

She cast her an encouraging smile then and urged, "Do go along upstairs straight away. On second thoughts, I shall accompany you myself and make certain it is done."

"How fetching you look," Lord Trenton told her when she came down to the dinner that preceded the soiree.

On this occasion Serafina knew he was being sincere, for she had marveled at the improvement in her appearance when she had viewed her reflection in the cheval mirror in her room. The gown of golden lace that Lady Betteridge had picked out for her was simply breathtaking and suited her coloring to perfection. It was high waisted and low necked, and the draped skirt fell into a short train.

After Bridie, her ladyship's maid, had undertaken some small alterations to the gown, all three of them had held their breath.

"Your hair is all wrong, though," Lady Betteridge then declared, disappearing from the room for several minutes before returning with a selection of hair ornaments.

Bridie dressed Serafina's hair into a style a little softer and more becoming than the one she usually wore, and her heavy curls were imprisoned into a golden net, the only adornment needed.

As she went into a curtsy before him, Serafina knew that Lord Trenton's admiration was something she would remember long after this masquerade was over.

He took her hand to raise her to her feet, asking in a low voice, "Are you nervous, Serafina?"

"A little," she admitted.

"You need not be. As my bride-to-be, no one will seek to harm you by words or by deeds."

She shivered slightly. "It would help alleviate my concern a little if I knew what you hoped to achieve by this flimflam."

He smiled enigmatically. "I wish I could be certain, ma'am, but at this point I cannot. At the very worst Lady Wolcot will be made to declare she was mistaken in her condemnation of you."

"Can you be absolutely certain of that?"

"I regret I cannot be certain of anything."

She cast him an annoyed look. "No doubt the uncertainty of this affair appeals to the gamester in you."

He fixed her with that dark fathomless gaze of his that so disconcerted her. "No one has ever accused me of gaming recklessly."

"I accuse you of being exceedingly provoking, my lord."

"The list of my awful qualities grows longer," he murmured as he put down his empty glass.

When dinner was announced a moment later, Serafina put her concerns to the back of her mind and tried to enjoy her new, albeit temporary, prominence. It felt rather odd to be seated so close to Lord Trenton, who appeared not in the least intimidated by the events he had instigated, conversing pleasantly to all those around him.

In fact, Serafina marveled at his ability to give his attention equally to all who sought it, and at the same time consume copious amounts of food. Try as she would, she still found it difficult to act the part of a female who had made a brilliant match, but she did manage to smile automatically as often as it was necessary for her to do so. Eating was a little more difficult, she found, especially whenever she caught sight of Jolyon, looking so very happy and knowing he had high hopes for all her new position would bring him.

The meal seemed interminable, but conversely Serafina thought it was over too soon and Lady Betteridge's invited guests began to arrive, most of them all a twitter in their anxiety to make the acquaintance of this nobody who they believed had carried away the greatest matrimonial prize in the beau monde.

As she was presented to each guest as they arrived by Lady Betteridge, Serafina curtsied, smiled, and accepted their good wishes for a happy future. Imogen, when she arrived at last, could not have been more excited if she had been the one about to announce her betrothal.

"I am bound to say that you do make such a handsome couple," she enthused, much to her friend's discomfort.

To save her the trouble of replying, Lord Trenton answered, "You are too generous, ma'am. Serafina casts us all into the shade."

"Oh, how gallant you are!" Imogen chuckled and went quickly to join Jolyon, leaving Serafina to face Lady Wolcot once more.

Unlike the other guests, the countess did not exude the kind of overt enthusiasm and ingratiating manner the others had shown, but she did contrive to smile nonetheless.

"Well, my dear, there is no doubt you have done very well for yourself, and I am pleased to see it. You always did seem to set yourself above the ordinary, which can be no bad thing if this is the result."

"You are very kind to say so, my lady," Serafina replied, not at all certain the countess had been flattering her.

"Miss D'Arblay, as you can see, does not wish to be on the outs with you, my lady," Lord Trenton quickly informed her. "She recognizes, and no doubt you do also, that a misunderstanding took place between you both and that must now be set aside for the sake of future harmony."

Lady Wolcot inclined her turbaned head. "You are full of good sense, my lord. I was just about to make a similar observation myself. I was, mayhap, a little hasty in my condemnation of you, my dear. I do hope you will not allow that to color your opinion of me for the future."

"Having you say so, my lady, is a great relief to me," Serafina replied in a strangled voice. "Imogen, as you may know, has been close for so many years, she is almost as a sister to me, which makes you also, in a way, kin." The countess looked somewhat taken aback, but taking her cue from Lord Trenton, she forced herself to continue, "I have, you see, such a small family of my own; it would be sad for me not to be on the best of terms with you."

Lady Wolcot continued to look confounded as she nodded her turbaned head, causing her feathers to shake uncontrollably. A moment later when she was greeted by an acquaintance, she took the opportunity of moving away.

Serafina's eyes filled with amusement as she watched her go. "If nothing more comes of this humbug, my lord, seeing her so humbled and contrite will have made it all worthwhile."

"It is evident she is unused to having the worst end of the stick, and it does not become her well. One thing is certain, she will no longer be able to cut you up to anyone in the beau monde. Any accusation she is likely to make now will be received with ridicule."

"I have no real desire to cause her embarrassment. That is all by the by, for my real wish is to clear my name of all taint."

When she saw Foster Stanway arriving with several of his cronies, she was somewhat taken aback and belatedly realized that Lady Betteridge had invited many of the people who frequented Wolcot House.

"Trenton, you have always displayed exemplary taste, and I have never admired it in you more than now," the dandy declared as he raised Serafina's hand to his lips. "Miss D'Arblay will make the most delightful bride."

"I cannot agree more, sir," was the viscount's urbane reply.

"It is a particular pleasure for me, Miss D'Arblay," Foster Stanway went on, "to be able to renew our brief acquaintance in such delightful circumstances as these. I was grievously disappointed when it appeared you had been obliged to return to the country. Indeed," he lowered his voice to a conspiratorial tone, "when I first heard of the . . . er . . . matter I felt moved to subject her ladyship to a severe setdown for her impetuosity toward you. I always maintained, you know, that the accusation was ill founded."

"I am truly indebted to you, sir," Serafina told him.

"Because of our differences on the matter, her ladyship and I did part brass rags, but now, naturally, she acknowledges that I was correct in my championing of your case."

On the arrival of more guests he was obliged to move on, and Serafina whispered to Lord Trenton, "I believe he did that a little too brown, don't you?"

Inclining his head toward her, the viscount answered in a voice only she could hear, "A high flyer if ever I heard one. He would not gainsay Lady Wolcot if she described Boney as a Chinaman." Serafina was obliged to suppress her laughter when he added, "Here comes Sir Walter Edgecombe. Be prepared to greet another toadeater."

"My dear Miss D'Arblay!" Sir Walter cried. "I always knew you were destined for great position. How kind of you to invite me to your little soiree. I feel quite humbled by your condescension."

"The pleasure is mine, sir," she responded wryly.

"Too kind," he murmured as he hurried away to greet the countess.

Mrs. Wilby arrived accompanied by Mrs. Renco and her gallant, all of whom were also often to be found at Lady Wolcot's house. Both ladies made appreciative remarks, although Serafina detected some manner of cynicism in their manner toward her.

When all the guests were assembled in the music room a little later, Imogen was invited to play the harp, which she did very well, much to Serafina's delight. Dottie Betteridge followed, playing the spinet, and then Serafina was asked to play the pianoforte.

Although she normally played well, it had always been before a very small group of people with whom she was well acquainted. Performing in front of such a large audience of strangers, including at least one who would be glad to see her look a goosecap, was to say the least, alarming.

However, she took her place at the pianoforte, and true to his word, Lord Trenton remained close to her all the while. When he insisted upon turning the pages of her music, no one else stepped forward to gainsay him, and as he acted the mooncalf for the purpose of their pretense, it was an enjoyable experience.

After the musical interlude was over, supper was served, and by this time, chattering to Imogen and Dottie Betteridge, Serafina began to relax at last. Her anxiety about the evening had stemmed from an ignorance of what it would bring. Perhaps, rather foolishly, she had been waiting for a flash of lightning, after which the guilty person would stand up and confess. That was if there was a guilty party. She realized all too well in a household like Lady Wolcot's, the snuffboxes could have been mislaid by a careless housemaid and were lying forgotten in some cupboard even now.

"When do you plan to be married?" Dottie was asking.

Serafina was startled out of her thoughts by so obvious a question. "Oh . . . we have not as yet discussed it."

Imogen smiled knowingly. "She does have the look of a mooncalf about her, I am bound to say. I have never seen you looking so radiant, dearest. Lord Trenton will make a much better husband than Squire Thornbury, you must own."

"Aunt Mira is very experienced at arranging wedding festivities," Dottie informed her. "Only last year she arranged a wonderful celebration for Polly, even though she only married the younger son of a baronet. Your wedding is bound to be the more splendid."

Serafina smiled but felt acutely discomforted, and Imogen confided, "I don't believe Serafina is yet accustomed to her new circumstances, Miss Betteridge."

"It has come as a great surprise—to us at least," the girl confessed. "I don't suppose either of you have ever visited Trenton Place."

"I don't even know where it is," Serafina confessed, knowing she was never likely to see it anyway.

"It is in Hampshire and is, I am bound to declare, the finest house in England."

"I shall look forward to visiting the estate once Serafina is married," Imogen enthused. "Rural house parties are always so pleasant, I find."

The embarrassing conversation was thankfully ended as far as Serafina was concerned by the setting up of the card tables. Many of the guests took their places, including Jolyon, which made her frown.

"Now, don't sell sous," he warned when he saw her expression.

"You know you should not gamble. You haven't the means."

"I am not exactly without a rag, you know."

"But you soon will be and, I'm afraid, likely to end up in dun territory. Most of these people are practiced gamesters accustomed to wagering huge sums with substantial incomes to fall back upon. You cannot hope to compete."

"I'm not a complete flat, Sal, so don't get into the hips on my account. I don't doubt that your husband-to-be will be glad enough to fish me out of the River Tick if I ever end up in it."

"Don't you dare even think of it!" she gasped.

He laughed at her outrage. "I'm only funning, dearest. You should be in high snuff, so don't act the damper with me."

"I just don't want to see you on the rocks, Joly."

"With m' sister about to marry one of the wealthiest men in the country, it's not likely, is it?"

Serafina suddenly looked agog. "Is he?"

"Is he what?"

"So plump in the pocket?"

Now it was her brother's turn to look surprised. "Don't you know?" She shook her head, and he added, gleefully, "You're about to marry a goldfinch, but I'm delighted to see it's not that which attracts you."

"Everyone appears to be plump in the pockets to me," she murmured, looking bewildered.

"Not so, I assure you. I am an example. Some of those present tonight—and I forbear to mention any names—are deep in dun territory."

Before she could make any further comment,

he went to join in the game of hazard, and with a troubled mind, this time on her brother's behalf, she went to watch Lord Trenton at his table. At least he could afford to lose, but he did game skillfully, not with the recklessness she had observed in others, and slowly but surely he began to win.

"You always have the devil's own luck," Foster Stanway told him as he threw in his cards and then, casting a sly look at Serafina, "Now it is evident to me why."

The viscount glanced at her, too. "Ah yes, I agree with you on that score, Stanway. Dame Fortune was with me when I won the heart of the fairest female in London, but my gambling success owes little to luck, I assure you."

"Oh?" the young man's eyes narrowed. "Are you able to share with us your secret, my lord?"

" 'Tis not a great secret, Stanway. Most gentlemen begin their gaming after eating prodigious amounts of food and imbibing hugely of their host's wine. My secret is a clear head and a light stomach. Try it, and you might discover it works for you, too."

He gathered up his winnings and, taking Serafina's arm, he led her away from the table, back into the drawing room where some of the guests were manning the instruments and playing for those who wished to dance.

"This has not been quite the ordeal I had anticipated," she confessed, and he merely smiled and invited her to dance.

Their every move was followed with great interest by most of the guests, Lady Wolcot in particular, and for this short time Serafina was able to enjoy her envied position as the future Viscountess Trenton.

# FOURTEEN

A little while later Serafina was delighted to see that Jolyon had abandoned the gaming tables and was dancing with Imogen. Glad as she was to see them enjoying each other's company, it was evident from her expression that Lady Wolcot was not in the least pleased by their closeness, and Serafina feared the girl would be obliged to suffer a setdown when she returned to Wolcot House.

Just then Serafina imagined how good it would be for the couple if she really was about to become Lady Trenton, how influential she could be on their behalf. Imogen would no longer be obliged to defer to Lady Wolcot in all matters.

"You must contrive to appear more light-hearted," Lord Trenton told her, and she knew she often did not look in the least happy as a bride-to-be should.

"My mind was dwelling upon another matter."

"Evidently it was one of some seriousness. Do you wish to discuss it with me?"

She smiled then. "Oh, no, for it is of no import whatsoever."

He glanced toward Imogen and Jolyon and said,

"When you first arrived, you warned me that Miss Geddes had already lost her heart."

She laughed uncomfortably. "I was angry because I felt that a couple who were so much attached could not be allowed to develop their relationship for social reasons. It seemed unjust to me."

His eyes narrowed. "Have you ever lost your heart?"

So startling was the question she almost stumbled. "Me?" She laughed in embarrassment and was about to deny that she had when she looked at him again. "Only the once, my lord."

"And the gentleman?"

"He was far too elevated for me."

"Obviously he was also a fool."

Serafina smiled sadly. "He never knew of my devotion."

"You should have told him."

"There seemed little point; he was attached to another."

On this particular occasion she was glad when the dance came to an end and grateful when Lady Betteridge beckoned her over.

"My friend, Lady Dangerfield, believes she was once acquainted with your mama."

After the initial introduction had been made, Serafina spent some time conversing with the lady, who was graciously condescending toward her.

A little while later she quailed when Lady Wolcot approached her. "Miss D'Arblay, you have impressed a good many people here this evening."

From the tone of her voice, Serafina gathered this

did not exactly please the countess. "Everyone has been exceedingly kind to me, my lady, and I am much obliged to them."

"It will not be long before you are able to dispense your own patronage to others. Do you relish the prospect, Miss D'Arblay?"

It was fortunate that Serafina was not obliged to answer for Lady Betteridge was once again beckoning, and as she made her excuses, the countess added, "You have a rare ability to ingratiate yourself, ma'am."

"I did not succeed in doing so with you, my lady," Serafina countered as she moved away.

"My dear," Lady Betteridge began as Serafina approached her, "would you be kind enough to go up to my room and fetch my shawl? I recall I left it on the bed when I came down, which is exceedingly crackbrained of me, for I have begun to feel a trifle chilled after the dancing."

As usual Serafina was happy not only to be of some service to Lady Betteridge but also to enjoy a short respite from her pretense, which immediately became a strain when anyone spoke of her coming nuptials, naturally a favorite topic of conversation.

She did not hurry, as she had come to understand no resolution of her problem was going to take place that night, and there was nothing to do save endure the remainder of the evening. She did wonder how she was going to reconcile herself to being a nobody again once the charade was over. One thing that would remain, she reminded herself with a slight shudder, was Lady Wolcot's malice.

When she approached Lady Betteridge's bedchamber, the door was already ajar, and Serafina could discern some movement within. Believing it to be Bridie, preparing her mistress's bed for the night, she went right in without pausing, only to draw back in surprise when she saw Foster Stanway bending over Lady Betteridge's jewel box that was standing open on the dressing table.

He snapped up straight when he heard her gasp of dismay, his cheeks growing ruddy. "Why, Miss D'Arblay, by all that's blue, what are you doing here?"

"I may ask the same of you, Mr. Stanway." She went farther into the room, anger welling up inside her like a spring. "What *are* you doing in Lady Betteridge's bedchamber?"

A wicked smile crossed his lips. "Would you really have me disclose a matter of such delicacy."

His remark only caused her anger to increase. "How dare you insinuate such a thing?"

"Just funning, Miss D'Arblay. In fact, I took a stroll and thought I heard a noise in here."

"What humbug!" she fumed. "It was you who stole Lady Wolcot's snuffboxes! Oh, I can scarce credit it possible, even now with the evidence so clearly before me."

He looked truly regretful. "I was at point nonplus, ma'am, in debt to the cent percents. You must see how it is."

"You're in the suds due to your own improvidence. Do not expect my pity when you have allowed me to shoulder the blame for your criminal activities."

"The last thing I expected was for you to be accused, you may be sure, Miss D'Arblay. Lady Wolcot took you in dislike, and you were the obvious felon in her eyes."

"You did nothing to redress the wrong."

He smiled artlessly. "How could I without condemning myself?"

"You muckworm!" she gasped. "You would have set the theft of Lady Betteridge's jewels at my door, too!"

She turned on her heel, for she could no longer bear to be in the same room as he. "Where are you going?" he asked, seeming concerned at last.

"To tell everyone of your perfidy, sir! Did you think I would not?"

"Hold hard, Miss D'Arblay. You are no green girl, so do not act in so hasty a manner. Only consider: I have taken nothing as yet, and by the time anyone arrives, I shall be back downstairs and denying I ever was here."

Serafina put one hand to her head. "You, sir, could easily hold a candle to the devil."

"I am just like you, Miss D'Arblay, unfortunate to be born without sufficient means."

"I do not take what is not mine!"

He gestured toward the jewel box. "Lady Betteridge is so full of juice, I'll wager she will not miss a few gewgaws."

"You are utterly beneath contempt, sir. Do you realize that if you do not confess to stealing those snuffboxes, I will be obliged to spend the rest of my life under the cloud of suspicion?"

"No, you will not," a familiar voice answered.

Wide-eyed, Serafina and Foster Stanway wheeled

around as the dressing-room door swung open, and Lord Trenton, followed by Sir Arthur and Lieutenant Buckler stepped out. The sight of them made Serafina gasp and then smile with relief. Foster Stanway's ruddy cheeks became ashen, and he stepped backward a few paces.

"What the devil . . . ?"

Lord Trenton was smiling grimly. "What the devil, indeed. We have heard and seen all, and you, Stanway, stand condemned with your own words."

"You are all dished up!" Sir Arthur added, look ing unusually severe.

"This was a trap," the young man realized at last.

"Just so," Lieutenant Buckler answered with grim satisfaction.

Serafina's heart swelled with gratitude and pleasure, so much so she had the mad urge to fling her arms about the viscount, only he was scarcely aware of her. His cold and furious look was directed toward Foster Stanway.

"I have a mind to curry your hide for what you have done," he told the cowed offender.

"Why don't you just call the constable and make an end of it?"

Sir Arthur touched his brother-in-law's arm to restrain him. "Just leave my house, Stanway. Don't let any of us set eyes upon you again, for it will go ill with you if we do."

Foster Stanway looked uncertain, and Lord Trenton added in a quiet but nevertheless resolute voice, "If we hear of property going missing in the future at any place where you are seen, we will know where to send the constable, sir."

The young man stepped backward, moving toward the door, and then, when he realized he was truly free to go, he began to run.

Serafina watched him go, and then Sir Arthur said to Lieutenant Buckler, "Let us follow and make absolutely certain he leaves the premises immediately."

When they had gone, Lord Trenton looked at Serafina at last. Tears of thankfulness trembled on her lashes, and a moment later she found herself in his arms. He held her close for a moment or two, and then, when she became aware of her impulsive action, in some embarrassment she drew away. He, however, did not seem inclined to relinquish his hold on her.

"How can I ever thank you for what you have done?" she gasped, trembling at the same time.

He looked down on her as she averted her eyes. "That is simple to answer, Serafina. If you truly wish to show your gratitude . . ."

"I do!"

"Don't cry off now your innocence is proved beyond doubt."

She gasped before she drew away to look at him. "I don't . . . understand."

"It is quite simple—allow our betrothal to stand. Marry me, Serafina."

A flickering smile of uncertainty crossed her lips. "I do appreciate your offer, but you must not think you need go to such extremes to spare me the humiliation of being given the go by."

He reached out and drew her back toward him. "Goosecap," he said fondly. "Didn't you realize I love you and probably have ever since the first time I saw you?"

"I thought you had fixed your interest with Imogen!"

"Only as a method of staying close to you. As you had already warned me that her heart was engaged elsewhere, I had no fears of causing her any anguish."

"I believe I loved you, too, from the start," she admitted.

"You looked so indignant with your hair flying in the breeze and your eyes wide with anger. How could I possibly resist?" he teased. "I've a mind to send it tumbling to your shoulders right now."

"You are outrageous!" she protested laughingly.

"And desperately in love for the first time in my life."

"Except for Elfrida, but it won't do. You know it won't."

"You have just declared your love for me! What can possibly stand between us now?"

"The most obvious thing," she answered with some difficulty. "I am a penniless nobody."

"You really are a peagoose, Serafina. I am neither penniless nor a nobody, so we are well matched. You have seen how you have been accepted already. All that remains is to place the announcement in the *Morning Post* with no further delay. Now, don't argue with me any further, for I have made up my mind to marry you, and I am accustomed to having my own way."

He kissed her then, and she protested no more. They remained entwined in each other's arms for some time until she asked breathlessly. "Did you suspect Mr. Stanway of the robbery before this evening, Robert?"

"Oh yes, I believed he was the guilty party for quite some time."

"That was exceedingly clever of you."

"I did come across a clue, I am bound to confess. You see, when I made my initial inquiries about the snuffboxes, I learned that some months ago an amount of jewelry had been stolen from the house of one of Lady Wolcot's cronies. Now, I could not establish who had been present on that evening, but I did know that Stanway was always at ebb tide, and it was not beyond the bounds of possibility that he and Lady Wolcot were present on the night of that particular robbery."

"I still maintain it was clever of you," she told him, looking at him admiringly, "but what if he had not been tempted to steal your sister's jewelry?"

"Knowing you would again be blamed? My dear, the temptation was too great, especially as his financial situation took a decidedly downward turn during our game this evening. I used whatever gaming skills I possessed to ensure he rose from the table with his pockets to let. Had I not succeeded, Arthur and Lieutenant Buckler had instructions to engage him in gaming until he was without a sous. It was not difficult, for he is a reckless gamester. All that remained was for us to follow him if he left the room, which he did. There is a door to the dressing room from the corridor. The gull-catcher had no notion we were there."

"I am full of admiration for all of you, not to mention my gratitude . . ."

"I did tell you at the outset I had a vested interest."

She dimpled. "It occurs to me that this trap could have been sprung just as easily without announcing our betrothal."

"We really needed a reason to bring him here. He is not usually to be found as a guest at either my sister's house or mine." His eyes suddenly had a twinkle in them. "However, you are in a way correct. I did ask you for the most selfish of reasons because I wanted to become closer to you."

"It was extreme behavior," she pointed out.

"It was necessary, for when you weren't closeted in the library, you did act very high in the instep, you know."

She laughed. "But you asked me to act out a masquerade."

"If I had asked you to marry me for real at that point, Serafina, I am afraid your pride would have prompted you to refuse, for all the countless reasons you have already mentioned."

As he gathered her into his arms again, she murmured, "Should we not return to the drawing room, dearest? After all, we are likely to be missed."

"I can assure you we shall not be missed. The news of our betrothal has just been superseded by a far greater sensation. As a hostess, my sister always provides the finest diversions for her guests. This evening is no exception."

Serafina chuckled and gladly gave herself up to

his embrace once again, responding to his kisses just as she wished to do.

Meanwhile downstairs Lady Wolcot, her attention attracted by the loud sound of running feet in the hall, looked bewildered as she watched Foster Stanway rush past the drawing room, followed close behind by Sir Arthur and Lieutenant Buckler.

"Where is Fos going in such a hurry?" she asked, "And why is Sir Arthur following him?"

"I rather believe he has been caught trying to steal some of our property," Lady Betteridge replied, coming up behind her.

The countess gasped as she wheeled around on her hostess. "Fos? Stealing? What humbug is this?"

"I regret to inform you, my lady, Mr. Stanway is the one who stole your snuffboxes and not Miss D'Arblay," Lady Betteridge informed her, unable to keep the satisfaction out of her voice.

"Oh, you cannot seek to gammon me!"

"I assure you I do not, my lady. I don't doubt by now there is undisputable proof. Mayhap if you had not been so prejudiced toward Miss D'Arblay, you might have come to realize it some time ago."

The countess's face grew deathly pale as blood drained from her cheeks. She tottered unsteadily and would have fallen if Lord Granton had not caught her and eased her onto the sofa. Several ladies who had been watching and listening avidly as the drama unfolded crowded around her, bringing out their fans and vinaigrettes to help the swooning woman.

Imogen squealed with delight as she turned to Jolyon. "Did you hear that, Jolyon? It was Foster

Stanway who stole the snuffboxes after all. Serafina has been vindicated at last! I always knew she would, but it is truly wonderful."

Jolyon stared at Lady Wolcot for a long while before he turned to his love. "I have a notion her ladyship might not have the heart or the will to bring you out next Season. My sister will be married by then, and she will be obliged to take you up. *She* is not likely to disapprove of me as your suitor!"

"Coming out is now of no account to me, Jolyon. I have come to realize I shan't enjoy being a debutante. All the others are so toplofty, and I never really had a fancy for anyone else but you, so there really wouldn't be any point in my making my debut."

He looked at her in astonishment for a moment or two, and then he smiled. "Do you think Sir Donald would not object if I offer for you?"

"How can he object to Lady Trenton's brother," she asked slyly, "for that is what you would be."

The young man smiled again. "Lady Trenton," he repeated. "Dash it all, Imogen, up until this minute I confess to you, I have not been able to think of my sister as actually betrothed to Lord Trenton."

"How foolish of you, dearest," she responded. "They are perfectly matched. Anyone can see that. I have known it from the outset, for when everyone believed his lordship was fixing his interest with me, all he wished to do was talk about Serafina!"

Lady Betteridge left the countess in the capable hands of several of her acquaintances as she came out of her swoon, murmuring, "Fos, Fos, how could you shame me so?"

Mirabel Betteridge slipped out of the room unnoticed and went quickly up the stairs, peering about her anxiously until she stopped outside her own bedchamber. The door was still ajar, and she could clearly see her brother and Serafina clasped in each other's arms and oblivious to the world around them. Lady Betteridge smiled with satisfaction and then just as quickly and quietly went back downstairs.

"I never did like that young man," one of her friends commented when she rejoined the guests in the drawing room. "There was always something decidedly havey-cavey about him."

"What a pity her ladyship did not think so," Mirabel Betteridge responded.

"The answer to that is simple; she has always been a goosecap. Well, you have truly provided a most diverting evening, Mira. Meeting Miss D'Arblay was novelty enough, but this is quite an extraordinary end to any evening I can ever recall. Your brother's wedding, by comparison, will be quite an anticlimax, I fear."

Lady Betteridge's eyes sparkled with mischief. "Don't imagine it will be so, my dear. Robert's wedding will be the most glittering anyone has ever seen! You have my word upon it."